W9-ARI-142

04/2016

City of Sin by Nana Ma[l...]

"You are infuriating and obstinate," [...]
muttered.

The hell she was. She poked him again. "You're a pompous jackass, so I guess—"

He shut her up with a hot, searing kiss. She should have seen it coming, but irritation had blinded her.

His strong arms wrapped around her, and his scent wove a hypnotic spell, seducing her, making it impossible to think.

Shipwrecked by Sienna Mynx

"What's your name?" he asked. His hand moved to hers and squeezed.

"Huh?" she answered.

"Your name is Huh?" he asked.

She laughed and shook her head no.

"Tell me your name, beautiful," he said. They were introduced just an hour before the wedding. He walked her down the aisle. Didn't he remember? When she considered it further, she recalled that besides the spilled drink incident, they hadn't spoken and were never formally introduced.

"Your [...] [...]er knees nearly [...] arm, and it exci[...]

"Deja[...]

"Ahh, Deja. Very beautiful.

PALM BEACH COUNTY
LIBRARY SYSTEM
3650 Summit Boulevard
West Palm Beach. FL 33406-4198

Nana Malone is a *USA TODAY* bestselling author. Her love of all things romance and adventure started with a tattered romantic suspense she borrowed from her cousin on a sultry summer afternoon in Ghana at a precocious thirteen years old. She's been in love with kick-butt heroines ever since. You'll find Nana working hard on additional books for her series. And if she's not working or hiding in the closet reading, she's acting out scenes for her husband, daughter and puppy in sunny San Diego.

Books by Nana Malone

Harlequin Kimani Romance

Wrapped in Red with Sherelle Green
Tonight with Sienna Mynx

Visit the Author Profile page at
Harlequin.com for more titles.

Sienna Mynx, bad-girl author of over thirty contemporary interracial romances, is acclaimed for her tales of torrid affairs between alpha heroes and the women born to tame them. Her stories awaken carnal desires and provoke laughter, soft sighs and gratifying tears of relief. Sienna's novellas reflect her thirst for romance told from a steamy, passionate perspective with the diversity women of all colors crave in erotic romance. She lives in southern Georgia.

Books by Sienna Mynx

Harlequin Kimani Romance

Tonight with Nana Malone

Visit the Author Profile page at
Harlequin.com for more titles.

Nana Malone
Sienna Mynx

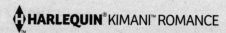
HARLEQUIN® KIMANI™ ROMANCE

If you purchased this book without a cover you should be aware that this book is stolen property. It was reported as "unsold and destroyed" to the publisher, and neither the author nor the publisher has received any payment for this "stripped book."

ISBN-13: 978-0-373-86445-4

Tonight

Copyright © 2016 by Harlequin Books S.A.

The publisher acknowledges the copyright holders of the individual works as follows:

City of Sin
Copyright © 2016 by Nana Malone

Shipwrecked
Copyright © 2016 by Sienna Mynx

Recycling programs for this product may not exist in your area.

All rights reserved. The reproduction, transmission or utilization of this work in whole or in part in any form by any electronic, mechanical or other means, now known or hereinafter invented, including xerography, photocopying and recording, or in any information storage or retrieval system, is forbidden without written permission. For permission please contact Harlequin Kimani, 225 Duncan Mill Road, Toronto, Ontario M3B 3K9, Canada.

This is a work of fiction. Names, characters, places and incidents are either the product of the author's imagination or are used fictitiously, and any resemblance to actual persons, living or dead, business establishments, events or locales is entirely coincidental.

® and TM are trademarks of Harlequin Enterprises Limited or its corporate affiliates. Trademarks indicated with ® are registered in the United States Patent and Trademark Office, the Canadian Intellectual Property Office and in other countries.

For questions and comments about the quality of this book please contact us at CustomerService@Harlequin.com.

Printed in U.S.A.

CONTENTS

To everyone who ever needs to let go a little.
Your fun is waiting.

Acknowledgments

Many thanks to my terrific editor, Glenda Howard,
and my fabulous agent, Natalie Lakosil, for bringing me
into the Harlequin Kimani Press family.

Dear Reader,

You know that saying, "What happens in Vegas stays in Vegas"? What if it doesn't? What if what happens in Vegas is love? Mortal business enemies Synthia and Tristan duke it out for their hearts and a job in one of my favorite cities. I loved writing this story because Syn is a woman close to my own heart, sometimes a little too serious. But when she lets go, the world is her oyster. The two of them are fun, snappy and unpredictable. I can't wait for you to meet them.

Always remember to Romance the Sass.

Nana

If you don't want to miss a single Nana Malone romance, make sure you join my reader group here: eepurl.com/blicGL.

CITY OF SIN

Nana Malone

Chapter 1

Tristan Dawson. Every woman's dream man in the looks department. Smart, sexy and oozing with charm. Too bad he was the enemy. And currently trying to charm his way into a project that was rightfully hers.

She was going to kill him. The single thing stopping Synthia Michaels from lining up her alibi was the whole prison thing. She was way too cute for an orange jumpsuit. As she glared at her nemesis, she plotted all the possible ways she could engineer his demise.

The jerk was *flirting* with the client. Okay, maybe flirting was a strong word, but he was certainly working his Tristan Dawson make-them-panties-drop smile. And with that smile, Syn felt her chances of landing this assignment slipping away.

From the moment Tristan started working at Stellar Reach as a market analyst, they'd been at odds, butting heads over client decisions and methodology. She loathed everything he stood for. *She* worked her butt off with painstaking attention to detail and serious work ethic. She couldn't deny it, his work was always done and it was difficult to find fault with the output. But his charisma and good looks gave him an unfair advantage. He'd poached some of her best clients with his effortless appeal. And God help the female clients. Syn turned her attention to Bella Bliss, Vice President of Marketing and Operations of Bliss Hotel Group, and almost felt sorry for the poor woman. Bella was a smart businesswoman, but here she was, salivating and stuttering over Tristan.

Not that Syn could entirely blame her. He was gorgeous. Tall and leanly muscled, he had a way of walking that made women stop and stare, imagining how good he'd be in bed. Couple the sheer sex appeal with his tanned skin and chiseled jaw, and most women around the office were goners.

On a regular day Tristan Dawson was hard to ignore, but in moments like this with him turning the full power of his allure on a client, the world was his. Syn was in no mood. She wanted this client.

She slid a glance over Tristan's heart-stoppingly handsome face and studied the way he smiled at Bella, as if she were the only one in the room. When he spoke, he was professional, but there was something about the way he talked and that rasp infused into his voice. It made Synthia's pulse race. Bella's too apparently, because the petite hotel magnate was staring at him as if he were the second coming of battery-operated boyfriends.

Bella Bliss leaned forward, her cropped double-breasted jacket giving the whole room an excellent view of her cleavage. Their boss, Bryan James, pretended not to notice. And if Syn was being fair, she'd have to give Tristan a medal for effort. As far as she could tell, he'd kept his gaze on Bella's eyes or at least in the general vicinity of her head.

Synthia also did her level best to ignore the blatant come-hither signals the hotel magnate was sending Tristan's way, but it was hard.

This was *her* client, and she wasn't about to roll over and let Tristan have it. No matter that the client was obvious about wanting him on the job. Bliss Hotel Group had been a long-standing client of Stellar Reach. It was standard practice to select the teams once the contract had been signed. It helped keep perspective fresh.

Synthia cleared her throat. "Bella, I'm thrilled about the opportunity to work with you again. I was part of the marketing and branding team for Bliss New York a few years ago."

Bella dragged her intent gaze from Tristan. "Oh, you were?"

Synthia nodded. "Yes. I was just an intern at the time, but I'm familiar with the Bliss brand."

Bella's gaze blinked into sharper focus as if suddenly realizing she was here for work and not for a date. She nodded, sending her fluffy blond curls shifting around her shoulders. "I'll have to review the work that was done on that. Since you have so much experience with the brand, you can bring Tristan here up to speed, Ms. Michaels."

Synthia didn't miss the familiarity Bella used with Tristan and the formality she used with her. In Bella's head, Tristan was already running the branding campaign.

Suck it up, Michaels. So what if Bella Bliss was looking at Tristan as if he were an ice-cream cone in the middle of a Santa Ana summer? She wasn't out of this yet. All she could do was her best. Lucky for her, on her worst day she could run miles around Tristan Dawson on his good day. She had this.

Tristan leaned closer to her, and her breath caught. For the most part, Synthia could ignore him, but when he turned those electric-blue eyes on her and made her the focus of all his attention, sometimes she forgot to breathe. But she was taking that little secret to the grave.

To make matters worse, he was silver-spooned, drove a BMW, and had the most sensual smile. Pretty much female kryptonite. And damn him, he knew it.

Syn tried to focus her attention on what Bryan was saying. Resolute, she kept her eyes on her laptop. But refusing to look at Tristan wouldn't help. He would still be there in all his sexiness staring at her, taunting her. To keep herself from temptation she dragged her eyes to Bryan as he spoke.

"As the two of you know, we've been working with Bliss Hotel Group for years. They want a full competitive research and branding package for their new hotel in Las Vegas."

A spike of adrenaline lit her blood, and her inner competitive nature stretched. She leaned forward and Tristan followed suit. God, the man was infuriating. He was always there. Always encroaching on her space. Syn kept her voice cool. "How soon do you want the research package?" As a senior market analyst for Stellar Reach, she excelled in market research for her clients. Identifying how to leverage what competitors were doing was one of her key strengths.

Bryan continued. "As you know, Bella's team will be breaking ground in eighteen months. They're looking for a full report on their lead competitors, the Decadence Hotel."

Bella chimed in. "In every city there's a Decadence,

there's also a Bliss. Over the years, we've been neck and neck for AAA Five Diamond Hotel ratings. With this new hotel, I want to blow them out of the water. So while you're at Decadence, you'll be posing as wealthy VIPs. We'll provide you with everything that a VIP package entails. When we purchased the package, we left room for play but made use of their concierge services to book tickets and dinners and clubbing experiences. You'll get to experience all that Decadence has to offer the elite crowd and you'll report back. What we're aiming for is information on their VIP experience that the average guest wouldn't even know to ask for."

Syn turned her attention to Bella, "I assume you still want the basics, the official room rates, the concierge, the facilities, the bottom line, their return on investment?"

She nodded. "Yes, of course. The bottom line is what it boils down to in the end. You'll be provided with the preliminary report we have on Decadence."

Tristan piped in, "While the bottom line is important, let's not forget the customer experience. Those who like to work hard like to play even harder. So I'll put that aspect into the report I compile."

Bella beamed. "I'm sure you will."

Syn chewed her lip. She'd worked on a Bliss Hotel campaign when she first started at the company. She wanted a real chance to prove herself now.

"Okay. If we get a team out there ASAP, we should be able to do some recon on the hotel and—"

Bryan held up a hand. "No team."

She frowned. "What do you mean no team? We need to get to work as soon as possible. In an ideal world we would have done this months ago."

Bryan smiled. "As usual, I appreciate your enthusiasm, Synthia, but *you're* the team. We're keeping it small this time."

She frowned. *What?* She was expected to work with Tristan? The management at Stellar Reach fostered an environment of competition. They believed that it brought the best out in their people. It forced teams to strive for great results for their clients, as well as work hard to keep them happy lest they lose the account to someone else. And it did force everyone to bring their A-game.

Tristan finally spoke and Synthia steeled herself against the raspy, hypnotic tone in his voice. "So, what do you need Syn and me for? Our approaches are completely different."

Bryan smiled. "I'm so glad you pointed that out, Tristan. Because the two of you complement each other."

Synthia's stomach rolled as she licked her lips. "I want to make sure I understand this right. You're sending the two of us to Las Vegas…together."

Her boss nodded. His ruddy cheeks going redder. "Yes. I believe the two of you bring some unique perspectives. You'll head out for the three-day weekend and then present your findings to Bella at the end of the month."

No. This couldn't be happening. She couldn't work with Tristan. He was disorganized. *Hot.* Brash. *Sexy.* A playboy. *It was clear he knew his way around a woman's body.* The bane of her existence. *The object of every fantasy she'd ever had over the past two years since he'd come to work at Stellar Reach.*

Synthia cleared her throat. "All due respect, Bryan, but Tristan and I have different methods. Perhaps in the interest of time, it would be best for Bliss to send just one of us. I have more experience with the account, but the choice, of course, is up to Bella." There was no way she was going to survive a weekend in Vegas with him.

She would spontaneously combust before they even got off the plane. Either that or kill him.

Bryan shook his head. "Normally, Synthia, you'd be right. Your styles are very different. But given our timeline and given that we need to see how the competition is doing, we need you both. Your skill sets will be a good match on this. Synthia, you'll focus on the bottom line. Check out pricing on rooms, activities and the like. You know the drill. See if you can find out their base costs. Tristan, I want you to focus on the services they provide. They are elegant but provide a fantasy element. And a very elite experience like what Bliss is trying to do. Both of you bring back your findings. From there, Bella will determine who will run the marketing and branding team."

Heading the marketing and branding team for a hotel like Bliss? That would be a huge career coup.

A client like that would be a shining star on her résumé. *And* if she did well, she could leverage it for a promotion in her next review. Plus, with the bonus, she could cover the entire last year of her sister's college tuition. As it stood, the payment for this semester was looming in a month, and thanks to footing the bill for last year's semester abroad, she was low. All she had to do was suffer Tristan Dawson for a weekend? *Done*.

She would just stay away from him. Wouldn't be difficult. Staying late and grinding wasn't his methodology. He said he worked better in the morning. They would just work separate schedules. It never ceased to amaze her how he'd risen though the ranks so quickly. He was haphazard and never took anything too seriously. His office looked like a war zone and he lacked finesse. But somehow the clients adored him. But he wasn't her prob-

lem. She knew what it took to succeed. And she had the
drive to get there. All Tristan had to do was stay out of
her way. She squared her shoulders. "When do we leave?"

Chapter 2

Three days with the ice princess. Tristan Dawson wondered who he'd pissed off to get that sentence. Fun wasn't in her repertoire. It would be like carrying an anchor around Vegas. Talk about a buzzkill. A *beautiful* buzzkill. But a downer nonetheless. It was a real shame too, because she might actually be fun if she ever loosened up a little.

From his first day at Stellar Reach, she'd fascinated him. Her reputation preceded her. She was tough and smart and got the best clients. Simply put, she'd been the one to beat. It didn't matter that he couldn't take his eyes off her. If he wanted to be considered on his merits and not his name, he had to give her a run for her money.

In the early days it had been difficult. She was always overprepared and came to win every time. It also didn't help that he'd spent the first two months struck stupid by her beauty. Her skin resembled melting chocolate and looked so soft he itched to touch her. Her dark, almond-shaped eyes dominated her face, complemented by high cheekbones and a beguiling smile. Granted, she'd never turned that soul-stunning smile in his direction, but he'd seen it before.

It hadn't taken long to learn that her nickname was synonymous with *aloof* and *cold*. Which was a real shame because her real name suggested otherwise.

Tristan closed his laptop. "If Synthia doesn't have a problem working with me, then I don't have one either." Except he'd be pretty much attached at the hip with her through the whole trip. Normally being partnered with a woman all weekend wasn't a hardship. He loved women. *All* women. But this one made him insane. Made him feel certifiable. He'd never met anyone more uptight. From day one, all he'd ever wanted to do was muss her up. Just once, he'd love to see her hair out of that bun and wild. The instant heat pooling in his gut made his skin flush. *Easy does it.* Thinking about how to get her hair wild and messy wouldn't do him any good. She already starred in too many of his dirty fantasies than were good for him. Not to mention that she'd flay him if she ever found out.

Their boss beamed at the both of them. "I'm glad the two of you are on board. Now, Synthia is more senior, so if any questions arise, just defer to her opinion. But I think you both can be our secret weapon on this contract, looking at both sides of the equation."

Once they were dismissed, Tristan followed Synthia out of the office. The moment they were out of earshot, he whispered, "I won't hold it against you that you just tried to toss me from the project."

She halted and turned her glacial, indifferent smile on him. "I'm sorry you see it that way. I was merely trying to save you from having to do any heavy lifting. I know how averse you are to that."

A spike of adrenaline hit him. There was no one he'd rather argue with. "Now, don't be mad just because I get to have some actual fun and you're stuck looking at the numbers."

She veered toward her office and despite his better judgment he followed. "Well, my idea of fun isn't to troll the Vegas strip clubs."

He let his mouth drop open and clutched his chest when they reached her office. "I'm wounded, Synthia. You think that I would stoop so low? I'm a classy guy. And I want only the best. I'd hire a private service to bring the girls to me." He winked at her.

"You're disgusting."

He grinned. He liked naked women as much as the next guy, but the whole strip club thing didn't do anything for him. If he was going to see a naked woman, there had better be touching involved. He mostly just liked to ruffle Syn's too neat, too perfect feathers. "You know, one of these days, you're going to have to tell me why you don't like me."

She directed her dark gaze on him. "It's not that I don't like you. It's that I'm indifferent. I do my best not to think about you ever."

God, she was impossible. "If you say so, sweetheart. You just keep telling yourself that. In the meantime, this trip to Vegas will be really fun."

She shrugged as if she couldn't give a damn. "As long as you stay out of my way, we'll be fine."

His hackles rose. "Honey, I have no intention of seeing you the whole time we're there." *Liar.* What he wanted to do was see sexy, mussed-up Synthia in Vegas.

She crossed delicate arms over her chest and drew in a deep breath. He almost high-fived himself for managing not to sneak a peek at her gentle curves. He didn't need that kind of torture through the rest of the day. "That will work fine with me." Her tight, brittle scowl morphed into that brilliant smile of hers and Tristan's brain shorted. Then she added. "Now, don't let the door hit you on the way out, Junior Warbucks."

She turned and walked to her desk as if she didn't give a damn whether or not he still stood there. Grinding his teeth, he left her office and didn't bother giving her the satisfaction of slamming it.

Back in his office, Drake Murphy, the head of Stellar Reach's legal team, was waiting for him with his feet kicked up on the coffee table.

"Make yourself at home why don't you, Drake?" Tristan mumbled.

His friend grinned. "Thank you, don't mind if I do." He inclined his head toward Synthia's office. "You and your girlfriend at it again? I could hear you from here."

"She's not my girlfriend." Tristan deposited his laptop onto his desk and sank into his chair.

Drake tossed a Nerf basketball at his head and laughed. "Oh, but you want her to be. It's like you're pulling her pigtails, man."

Tristan cracked his neck and tossed the basketball smoothly into the hoop mounted on the wall. "I don't want her." He impressed himself with how smoothly the lie flowed off his tongue. He was ready to claw his skin off, he wanted her so bad.

Drake laughed. "I swear, the two of you bicker like crazy people. I honestly wish you two would just hit the sack and get it over with already. It's hard to watch."

"Never going to happen." Tristan narrowed his eyes. "Excuse me, aren't you legal? Should we even be discussing this?"

"I left my legal hat at the door. Do I need it?" Drake studied his friend.

"Not that I know, but she might glare me to death. No matter what I do, she's not warming up to me."

Drake nodded. "Well, that's because you're an idiot."

Tristan laughed. "Only sometimes."

"You ever planning on doing anything about that?"

"Like what?" *Kissing her until she melts in my arms?*

Drake tossed another Nerf ball at his head and Tristan caught it one-handed. "You know, asking her out like a grown-up. Since that's what you really want to do. This whole acting-like-a-jerk thing isn't going to get you anywhere."

"It's not like I'm doing it on purpose. She's immune to my charm. The woman hates me."

Drake shrugged. "Well, maybe if you stopped poaching her clients she might like you better. I don't know about you rich boys, but for us common men, when we hit puberty we got the lesson that girls like it when you're nice to them."

Tristan shook his head. "I'll try to remember that when I'm stuck with the she-devil in Vegas."

Drake blinked at him. Then blinked again. "You're going to Vegas with her?"

"Yeah, to do recon for Bliss."

A low roar of laughter spilled out of Drake. "Oh, man, this is going to be good."

"Yeah, good for you. One of us is going to need a lawyer after we declare war on each other. It's going to get crazy."

"Maybe you try being nice to her." Drake winked as he stood. "Might even throw her off her game. She's been on the Bliss account before. She's going to fight you hard for this one. You'll need every advantage you can get."

The one thing Drake didn't know about Synthia was that she always fought to win, Bliss account or not. "Yeah, I'll give it some thought."

Tristan's desk phone rang as his friend meandered out of his office. He answered with a brusque "Dawson."

There was a brief pause and the hairs on the back of his neck stood. "Tristan, it's your father."

His stomach pitched. As if he couldn't recognize the old man's voice. "Dad…everything okay?" How long had it been since they'd seen each other? Six months maybe? Since his sister Tawny's last birthday. And even then, they'd avoided each other and said as little as possible.

The old man cleared his throat. "Yes, everything is fine. I'm calling about Taylor's congratulatory dinner for his promotion. It's this weekend."

Hell. Yet another reason to be a disappointment. "Sorry, Dad. Can't make it. I'll be out of town."

"This is important, Tristan. Your brother just became a vice president. You can put off whatever vacation plans you have."

Tristan gritted his teeth. "It's for work, Dad."

His father harrumphed. "Work? That place you go every day hardly qualifies as work."

And there it was. It had taken less than a minute for his father to tell him that he wasn't living up to his potential. "If this conversation is veering toward you telling me to come back and help run Dawson Incorporated, then we don't have anything else to talk about. I have no desire to be an investment banker."

"Why do you insist on being so stubborn? This is your legacy."

"I would rather have something I earned. You taught me that all that money comes with strings I'd rather not have attached, so if this is you asking nicely, then I'm going to have to politely decline."

"You are so irritatingly stubborn and childish. All I asked was that you heed my advice, and you walked away from this family."

The knot of anger increased even as it grew tighter. "Is that how you remember it? I remember it differently." When he'd told his father he didn't want to work at the investment firm, the old man threatened to cut him off.

"Don't act like a child. I can pull you home whenever I want. Do you really think that you're insulated in your little job? If I want, I can come in and buy that place. You will have to learn eventually that I am in control. I can fight to get control of your trust fund."

"That's where you're wrong, Dad. We're done." Tristan hung up with a soft click of the phone. It didn't matter how much his father got to him. The old man wasn't his puppet master. He'd fought hard for his independence and he was going to keep it. And that meant landing this account. Even his father couldn't ignore the prestige of the position. All he had to do was beat Syn for it.

"That man is a pain where the sun don't shine. He's insufferable and a jackass."

"Don't forget smoking hot, because let's face it. He is."

Synthia scowled at her best friend, Olivia Banks. She and Liv had been friends since they started at the company as interns over five years ago. Synthia could always count on her friend to give it to her straight. "Try to keep up, Liv. We hate him, remember?"

Liv put up her hands and laughed. "Oh, honey, I remember. He is our sworn enemy and we have to make him suffer. *But* that doesn't preclude us noticing the assets on hand." She waggled her eyebrows.

Syn rolled her eyes and plopped into her chair. "I swear, you're almost as bad as he is."

Liv clapped a hand to her chest. "Now, I take offense at that. I might ogle and appreciate, but I don't use my..." She paused and reconsidered. "Okay, so maybe I've used my gifts for evil before, but Tristan Dawson takes it to a whole new level."

Synthia bit back a chuckle. "You're impossible, you know that?"

Liv grinned. "Funny, I've been told that before."

Synthia let the tension roll out of her shoulders. "I swear, you should have seen his smug face. With his magnetic smile and his focused attention, Bella didn't stand a chance. She was all fluttering eyelashes and breathy voice by the time Tristan freaking Dawson was done with her. She'd been Dawsoned." Liv had coined the phrase when he started at the company two years ago to describe how most of the women in the company reacted when Tristan graced them with a smile. Except Syn.

"So, what are you going to do about it?"

Synthia raised an eyebrow. "What makes you think I've got a plan?"

"Because. This is you we're talking about, so rolling over and playing dead is not in your nature. You're too stubborn and good."

"Thanks for the vote of confidence, Liv, but I'm a little worried about this one."

Liv frowned. "Why?"

"Because of Tristan. You know they're sending us to Vegas. I just know he's going to use this opportunity to his advantage. I'm getting the impression from Bella Bliss that she's more interested in what Tristan can provide her in the bedroom than what I can provide her for the hotel."

"Then why don't you fight fire with fire?"

Syn frowned. "I don't understand."

"Hear me out. Tristan is already using his charm to his advantage. Your best traits are your brain and your tenacity, which you have in spades, but you have an ace in the hole."

Syn laughed. "Oh, really? What's this ace? Do I have a magic wand that will make Bella pay attention to the facts and figures when I present?"

"You can call it a magic wand, I'll just call it your banging bod."

Syn raised her eyebrows. "Um, I don't think Bella's into chicks, Liv."

Liv shook her wild mane of red hair. "No. It can't have escaped your notice how Tristan looks at you. There's interest there."

"Um, in case you haven't noticed, we can barely stand to be in the same room with each other. It'll be a wonder if we both make it back from Vegas in one piece." She pointed a finger at her friend. "In case there's any doubt, I'm the one who'll be burying a body."

Liv giggled. "Of that I have no doubt, but take me seriously. All you have to do is play nice with Tristan and he'll be too busy focusing on you to focus on his work. You'll have the whole thing in the bag before he knows what hit him."

Flirt with Tristan? *Yeah, no.* Didn't matter that the thought alone made the butterflies flutter low in her belly. "Not going to happen. I'm getting this account all on my own."

Liv groaned. "Honey, I'm not suggesting you sleep with the guy, but if you do, please take detailed notes and let me live vicariously. I'm just saying throw him off his game a little. Right now he's in there with his boy, planning your takedown. Do you or do you not remember the Boyd account?"

Syn ground her teeth. Boyd Seduction had been her account for over a year. But one chance encounter between Tristan and the lingerie designer's CEO and Syn was off the account and out that bonus check. Her work was better than his, but there was a certain kind of client that liked his demeanor. That kind wanted to have a personal connection. And while she was hardworking and well liked, everyone *loved* Tristan. *Except you.*

"I can't do it, Liv. Besides, don't you think Tristan will see that coming from a mile away? He's not dumb."

Liv sighed. "Honey, the amount of time that man spends looking at you, he won't be thinking at all." She winked. "Besides, I'm just asking you to be nice, throw him off. Meanwhile, you're getting together the best presentation Bella Bliss has ever seen."

Okay, this was getting out of hand. "First of all, Tristan doesn't look at me." But just the idea of it made her body flush with heat. Tristan Dawson was the stuff of really hot, need-battery-operated-boyfriend inducing dreams. With his broad shoulders and teasing grin, it was no wonder.

Liv raised a delicately arched eyebrow. "Babe, if you believe that, then I have a bridge to sell you. What you have to ask yourself is, how badly do you want this account?"

She didn't have to ask herself that question. She already knew she'd do whatever it took to get the Bliss account. Even if it meant cozying up to her nemesis.

Chapter 3

Three whole minutes into his trip with Synthia and Tristan was ready to call uncle.

By the time they boarded the plane, his nerves were raw. *It's only three days.* Yeah, maybe, but he was pretty sure someone would catch a legal case before the weekend was up.

The car service had picked him up first, and when they'd gone to her house to get her, she already looked irritated to see him. Granted, he'd poked the dragon when he replied to her "Good morning" with "I've always wanted to see the natural habitat of an ice queen." She'd rewarded him with a scowl. And so it had gone the rest of the way to the airport. Him teasing her, and her resolutely ignoring him while managing to shoot him daggers with her eyes.

He watched her struggle to stash her carry-on bag in the overhead bin for a moment before offering to help.

Standing and leaning over her petite frame, he stabilized the bag.

"No, it's okay, I really don't need your help. I have
it—"

The rollaway slipped again as a bottle of water escaped
the side holder and rolled down the cabin. But then the
bag gave way, bringing her body into direct contact with
his, and they both froze.

He knew enough to hold his breath. The strawberry-
scented hair product she used was enough to give him a
hard-on for a week. He didn't need to inhale that while
he was in close proximity to her.

Syn wobbled in her heels and he placed his hands on
her hips to steady her. *Big mistake.* Touching? What kind
of idiot was he? But even though his brain gave the com-
mand, he didn't let go. When he managed to force the
words out, they tore from his chest. "You okay?"

She nodded but didn't move for several breaths. Every
sharp inhale brought her butt into tighter contact with
his throbbing erection. *Torture.*

She turned in his arms, glancing at him from half-
lowered lids. "Yeah, fine. Thanks."

Something was wrong with this picture. Her pupils
were dilated and her voice was breathy. Her tongue
peaked out to moisten her lips and he bit back a groan,
promptly letting go of her waist. She wanted him too.

Syn could ignore him. Hell, she *would* ignore him. It
couldn't be that hard. Never mind that she'd been locked
in a flying tin can with him for the better part of an hour
from Los Angeles to Vegas and his subtle musky cologne
had started to weaken her defenses.

The blinding lights of the Strip dragged her focus from
him as the limousine turned toward the hotel. "Wow."

"You're screwing with me."

When she turned to face him again, Tristan was staring at her. "What?"

"You look like you've never seen the Strip before."

She shrugged. "That's because I haven't."

"How is it that a woman named Syn has never been to Vegas? Surely you've had some debauched girls' weekend or something."

She set her jaw. There wasn't a lot of time for fun weekends when she had her sister to look after. "I'm always working. One of these days I'll come just for fun." Yeah, like when she didn't have to worry about Xia's tuition.

"It's a shame. Even *you* have to have fun sometime."

Her mouth dropped when they pulled up to the circular drive of the hotel. Decadence really had pulled out all the stops. The driver opened the door for them, and Synthia stared up, speechless. Thankfully her brain automatically shifted into work mode, and she turned on record on her phone so she could make impromptu notes as they went.

Behind her, Tristan chuckled. "I bet you were one of those nerdy girls who sat up front and took careful notes, weren't you?" His breath whispered on the back of her neck and she shivered.

She gave him a bland smile over her shoulder. "I'm surprised you were ever in class long enough to notice them. Didn't they excuse jocks from class in your college?"

He smirked. "I was Honor Society, actually." Then he shrugged and added, "And quarterback."

She rolled her eyes. "Of course you were. Look, let's just stay out of each other's way while we're here. I'm sure that will be easy enough. I'll do my thing and you'll do yours."

"Fine by me, Princess. And if you need me for anything at all…" He slid his gaze over her, lighting little blazes everywhere his gaze landed. "Just look for where there are people having fun."

"I won't be looking for you."

He smirked. "Sure you won't."

The gold-ribboned black marble reflected the light from the hanging chandeliers in the lobby. Synthia looked up and the crystal shimmered with rainbows of bounced light. Given the sheer number of guests for the grand opening, it should have felt crowded, but the lobby still seemed expansive, yet somehow warm. Greek gods of old were carved into the expansive pillars lining both sides of the lobby, and a massive statue sat in the center with an ornate water fountain surrounding it. Thanks to the lights in the fountain, the water appeared a deep burgundy color. As if mimicking wine. Maybe the center figure was supposed to be Bacchus, the god of wine and intoxication. She snuck a glance over at Tristan and he grinned. Of course. This was exactly his kind of place. There was an energy and a humming vibe of life that probably spoke to someone like him.

There were several sitting areas decorated with understated opulence. The furnishings were modern and simple, but the rugs were Aubusson and as decadent as the hotel's name would suggest. The clientele was classy, wealthy. Clearly had money. But they were young. Tallying the average age of the guests milling around the lobby, she would have said no more than thirty-five. They were young with disposable income. These were not the young family types, though. More like young professionals looking to unwind.

Bella Bliss really had pulled out all the stops to get the lowdown on her competition. Syn and Tristan had VIP access to tonight's opening of Excess Club and Lounge. Synthia had never been to Las Vegas before and even she had heard buzzing of the new, about-to-be-it bar. Rumor was tonight's event was supposed to be star-studded with movie stars.

Synthia wasn't usually one for parties, but she was actually looking forward to it. If she was lucky, she might have a celeb sighting. Xia would be pea green with envy. Not her thing, personally, but she told herself she owed it to her sister to at least try to enjoy the experience even though she was stuck with Tristan.

At the check-in desk, she handed over her ID. All she wanted was a hot bath and a chance to get to work in some peace and quiet. First things first, she'd ask for a tour of the rooms, then get a hold of the concierge and make nice. She already had her cover story. Looking for an upscale bachelorette weekend venue. That should get her access to all the ballrooms and conference rooms.

The pretty blonde behind the reception desk smiled at her warmly. "Welcome to Decadence. I hope you enjoy your stay here."

"Thank you." She smiled. "I'm sure I will."

From beside her, Tristan stared. "Is that a Synthia Michaels smile? I've heard tell of such a thing, but you know I've never experienced it for myself, you see."

"I smile. Just not at you."

He just laughed.

The blonde handed over her keys. "There are two keys in here for you and Mr. Dawson. If either of you should lose these, just come back to the front desk and we'll replace them free of charge. Since your room is one of the penthouse suites, you'll take the private elevator, located…"

Synthia blinked. "Wait a minute, did you say the keys for me *and* Mr. Dawson?"

The blonde nodded.

She shook her head vehemently. "Oh no, there must be some mistake."

On this, she and Tristan were united. He dropped his voice low and leaned forward. The poor girl behind the counter didn't have a chance. Synthia knew how hard it was to concentrate with those electric-blue eyes pinned on you. "Now, what did you say your name was again?"

The woman licked her lips. "It's, um, it's Lisa."

He turned the charm up a notch. "Pretty name. Listen, I think there's been a mistake, Lisa." The way he said her name sounded husky and seductive and the poor girl flushed bright red.

Synthia barely managed to refrain from hitting him. After all, her future rested on his ability to flirt their way into *two* rooms.

Lisa gave a nervous smile. "I'm sorry, but you're booked in the south-facing penthouse suite. It's got a great view of the Strip."

He frowned and leaned in even more as if they were conspirators and he didn't want anyone hearing their conversation. "I think we're supposed to have separate suites."

Lisa shook her head, wavy locks swinging over the shoulders of her jacket "I'm sorry. I wish I could move you, but it's opening weekend. We don't have anything else available."

Not happening. Synthia needed space from Tristan, not *more* alone time. Alone time was trouble. He'd already gotten a glimpse of her emotions when he looked into her eyes as he'd helped her with the suitcase. He'd known then. No doubt he'd use it to his advantage.

The idea was to throw *him* off his game. Not the other way around. This was her chance to shine with her work.

She snatched the key off the counter with a smile. "Thank you for your help, Lisa." She strode away as quickly as her heels would carry her. Maybe Tristan would get another room. Maybe he'd find some rich heiress to shack up with. All she knew was she was taking the best bed and the bathroom.

It turned out she wasn't that lucky, because he followed closely on her heels. "Going somewhere, roomie?"

"Oh, I'm so sorry, Tristan. I thought you were headed for the fun. Some of us have to work."

He slid into the elevator and swiped his key over the magnetic pad before pushing the sole button.

They both kept to their corners as they were carried up to their room. When the car dinged again, and the doors opened, Synthia froze. As the doors slid open, a gold and marble foyer presented itself. "Holy hell," she whispered. Sure, she'd stayed at luxury hotels before, but the detailing was exquisite and there was a solitary sculpture located in the middle of the room that just screamed *priceless*.

Tristan whistled low. "Looks like Bliss wasn't kidding about the VIP treatment."

"I understand why it's one suite now," she muttered. The rest of the suite was decked with contemporary furnishings and modern art on the walls. The living room was the size of her whole apartment. Even the kitchen was extravagant. They had the latest appliances and the same marble from the foyer flowed into the kitchen detailing too.

On the far side of the living room, there was a large balcony with a pool view. "It's beautiful," she whispered.

At first he didn't say anything, but she could feel him staring, so she met his gaze. He seemed puzzled.

"What?" She frowned.

He quickly shook his head. "Nothing. I'd never seen that look on your face before until today."

"What look?"

"Wonder. It's pretty stunning."

With that simple statement, Synthia knew she was in more trouble than she'd bargained for.

Chapter 4

Synthia adjusted the cap sleeves of the black dress and studied herself in the mirror again. Not bad. She'd styled her hair down, adding big voluminous curls. It gave her a sultry look. Her earrings were understated diamond studs and she wore a simple diamond solitaire. As for the dress, it had a conservative scoop neckline but was also completely backless.

Once she and Tristan had settled in, she'd buckled into work while he went to check out the pool. She'd requested one of the staff to show her some of the other rooms and she'd managed to get some pictures. She'd also done a rate analysis of Decadence room packages. Now the two of them were due at the hotel's swanky lounge.

But despite several attempts, she couldn't open the door of her room and face him. *It's not like it's a date. Be brave, Syn. He's just a man.* She could handle him. Just as Olivia said. But when she opened the door to the suite, Tristan was nowhere to be seen. The light in his bedroom was on, so she could only assume he'd come back at some point while she was working. Question was, was he still there, or had he already left? Without her? As quickly as the sting of rejection flared, she shut it down. It wasn't as if they were here on some romantic getaway. She was here to work. She certainly couldn't expect him to wait for her.

The balcony door was open and she couldn't help a peek at the Strip. She'd secretly always been fascinated by this city even though she'd never been here. For all its garishness and debauchery, there was still something glamorous and exciting. It made her blood hum.

"Hot damn." The muttered curse had her whirling around. Tristan, decked in an impeccable tuxedo, stood staring at her.

"What's the matter?"

When he still didn't say anything, she shifted uncomfortably. Maybe she should have brought something nicer. That was the problem with doing these types of events, finding something that didn't label her as the impostor she was. But she hadn't really owned anything ritzier for this party.

Tristan opened his mouth, shut it and then tried again. "N-nothing. You look...er...nice. You look nice."

Syn studied him. He seemed sincere. But then you never did know with Tristan. He was too slick. Too practiced at the art of charm. And he looked too good in that tux. She tried to remind herself of what Olivia had said. Use some of his skills against him. *Be charming, be nice to him.* When it came to Tristan, she was far more practiced at sarcasm, but she would try nice for a change. "Thank you. You clean up pretty nice yourself." He'd shaved and for the first time since she'd met him, his jaw was smooth. Her fingertips itched to touch his handsome face, but she wisely kept her hands to herself.

He did a little twirl and grinned. "This old thing?"

She couldn't help laughing. When she did, he stopped and stared at her again, his gaze intense. "You should laugh more often."

Well, what exactly was she supposed to say to that? "Well, I laugh when I find something funny. And right now your catwalk chic coupled with your Blue Steel expression is pretty funny."

His voice pitched lower. "So, what do you say, Syn? Want to go to a party?"

Tristan knew how to handle women. He'd been doing it all his life, but when it came to Syn, he immediately morphed into a gawky teenager with bumbling hands and fumbled words. But tonight was especially bad.

That backless number by far was the sexiest dress at the party. Oh, sure, some voluptuous women were showing more skin or their attire was so elaborate that her dress seemed simple in comparison, but when she turned around, everybody stared. The fabric skimmed low and stopped just at the top of the curve of her gorgeous ass, tantalizing him to touch it.

Her back was strong, as evident by the sleek muscle on display, but she was also soft. Half the night he wanted to reach out and skim her spine with his finger. Would she shiver? Would her pupils dilate as they had done on the plane? Would she part her lips for him?

Earth to Tristan. Get a grip.

Silently he searched the crowd further and found her on the balcony, a glass of champagne in her hand. Every time he looked up and found her, she was alone. When he'd seen her standing in their suite with the moonlight bringing out the highlights in her hair, she'd looked like an angel. A sexy angel sent to drive him insane.

Chapter 5

Every woman in the world knew when a man was watching her. And right now Synthia could feel Tristan's burning gaze on her back. *Well, let him stare.* If it meant he was distracted from work, then better for her.

A waiter moved by with a full tray of champagne, and she took one. She was working, but the whole point of the party was to have some fun. Or at least do a reasonable facsimile. In the meantime, she'd already cataloged what they were serving, the brand of champagne they offered and who they were using for the DJ and dancers. She could tally costs later for her presentation.

"A beautiful woman, all alone with a view like this, is a travesty."

The voice behind her was smooth and mellow and she turned with a smile and studied her new companion. No doubt, he was handsome. Whereas Tristan's hair was dark, this guy was blond. He had the same lean, rangy build, but Tristan was taller. And this guy's eyes were dark like warm chocolate.

But he's not Tristan. Yeah, that was for sure.

"Um, thanks but I'm good."

His smile made him even more handsome. He made a pretty picture and he knew it. "Oh, come on, I don't bite, and I think you're stunning. I'd like to get to know you a lot better." He slid another step into her personal space and Syn resisted the urge to back up. Clearly he was gorgeous, but she just wasn't interested. She already had one too-pretty-for-his-own-good man who haunted her dreams; she didn't need another.

"Oh, you're good. But just how many women have you used that line on tonight?"

He grinned. "Well, so far just you, but I'm hoping to have a high success rate with it."

Syn laughed and cocked her head. "Oh boy, that's a lot of pressure on a girl. I don't want to mess with your average."

"Then don't disappoint me," he said with a tilted head and a grin. "Let me buy you a drink."

She held up her glass. "Already got one."

"Fair enough, then let me buy you diamonds, emeralds, whatever you want. Anything so I can spend some time with you."

She shifted her hip. "You think I can easily be bought, do you?"

His gaze slid lazily over her body. "Not easily, but I'm willing to try."

She laughed. "As appealing as that sounds, no, thank you."

He clutched a hand over his chest. "You're breaking my heart. I haven't even tried my best lines yet."

"You're better off trying them on someone else.

There's a brunette by the door and she's been eyeing you for the last ten minutes."

He sidled up to her. "But she's not you, is she?"

Suddenly a shadow loomed over her. She didn't need to turn around to know that it was Tristan. Her body set off the internal alarm it always did every time he was close. He slung an arm over her shoulder and kissed her on the cheek. Her body seized from the shock and the hot spear of need.

"Sorry, I got distracted, darling. I hope the champagne's okay. I can get you something else if you want."

Unable to move her limbs, she forced herself to inhale deep. The hint of musk and ocean breezes swirled around her. When her brain finally came online again, she turned to stare at his arm pointedly, then back at his face. Either she was too subtle or he deliberately ignored her reproachful glare.

Tristan turned to her companion. "Who's your friend, Syn?"

The guy put up both his hands. "No harm intended. Just having a conversation." He beat a hasty retreat.

Because she wasn't interested, she let him scamper away, but the moment he was out of earshot, she stepped out of Tristan's hold. "Just what the hell do you think you're doing?"

"Here's a hint, sweetheart. Where I'm from, when someone rescues you, it's customary to say thank you."

She crossed her arms and raised an eyebrow. "Who said I needed your help?"

"Oh, come on. It was clear you weren't into him. The only person who didn't know that was *him*."

It would be a snowy day on Venus before she thanked him. "For your information, I can take care of myself, Ricky."

He frowned. "Ricky? I'm Tristan, remember?" he said cheekily.

"Ricky Schroder. I didn't need you to ride in on your little train. This isn't an episode of *Silver Spoons*."

He shook his head. "You know what? Next time, I'm going to leave you to fend for yourself."

She placed her glass on the cement ledge before she gave in to the urge to throw it in his face. "I'd appreciate that. That guy was probably taking his lessons from watching you hit on woman after woman all night."

Tristan grinned and she cursed the butterflies. Her body warmed and heat pooled in her core. "If that were me, I would have recognized a lost cause."

A lost— She spoke through clenched teeth. "Oh, so I don't fall for your phony charm, and *I'm* the problem? I've had enough for the night. Dealing with morons has a way of exhausting me."

She had made it only about a hundred feet before a strong hand wrapped around her upper arm. "Where are you going? Not that I care about your presentation, but I know you. You'll find a way to blame me because you didn't get all the information you needed."

Syn dragged her arm back. "You worry about your own presentation. Unlike you, I don't lose."

If she thought she was going to manage to escape him in the elevator, she should have thought twice.

Using his key fob, he hit the button for their floor before rounding on her. "What is your problem with me anyway? From the moment I started at Stellar Reach you've been riding me."

Oh, hell. She *would not* think about riding him. She *would not* think about riding him. She *would not*— Oh, there it was, an image in her mind of them on the floor, naked and writhing, with her riding him to orgasm.

She pointed a finger in his chest. "I take offense to how you do things. You think with a pretty smile you can get whatever you want." She jabbed him. "I worked my butt off on the Boyd campaign and you just strolled in with your connections and your smile and pushed me off my own project, and that wasn't the first time. And I wouldn't even have had a problem if I'd seen you put in any actual work on that. Instead you relied on your ability to pal around to get that client."

He leaned into her jabbing finger and bracketed his arms against the elevator wall on either side of her head. "You're still pissed about that? You really need to let things go. It's not like you haven't stolen clients from me before. Does the Travers account mean anything to you?"

She narrowed her eyes at him and poked him again. "It's not called stealing if you actually do all the groundwork and the client chooses you."

"That was my first time I had a shot as a lead and you swooped in with your charts and your graphs. You are such a pain in the—" He muttered something unintelligible through ground teeth.

"Likewise." With the both of them squaring off and breathing hard, with only a scant two inches between their bodies, Syn knew definitively how this weekend would end. With only one of them still standing.

"You are infuriating and obstinate," Tristan muttered.

The hell she was. She poked him again. "You're a pompous jackass, so I guess—"

He shut her up with a hot, searing kiss. She should have seen it coming, but irritation blinded her.

His strong arms wrapped around her, and his scent wove a hypnotic spell, seducing her, making it impossible to think.

His tongue slipped between her lips and she moaned.

He tasted so good. *Oh. My.* When her brain started to process, her first thought was *Holy moly, Tristan Dawson, sex god to the world, is kissing me.* The next, as he expertly slid his tongue over hers: *Oh, hell. He could give lessons.*

Tristan backed her up against the wall as he growled low in his throat. Hands on either side of her head, he nipped at her bottom lip. Syn hesitated for only a second before her arms looped around his neck into his hair. When she twined her fingers into the silken locks, he groaned and deepened the kiss.

Her body was a bundle of raw nerves and he knew just how to stroke every, single, one. It was as if each rational, thinking brain cell she had stood by on the sidelines gawking as her body and its need took over the helm.

He braced her against the wall and urged her legs around his waist. They both moaned as that brought her heated core in contact with his pulsing erection.

For once, Syn took a vacation from her overanalytical brain. She took a vacation from good sense. All she wanted to do was feel. To be desired and for once to throw caution to the wind. For once just take the pleasure that was offered without thinking it to death a million times.

For that elevator ride, she went on a ride with Tristan Dawson. Not only did he devour her lips; he treated her mouth like a delicacy, tasted and tempted and teased her tongue into playing. She wanted this. Wanted him.

As he licked into her mouth with his hot tongue, he slid a hand up her stomach and ribs. He paused just short of touching her breast and Syn whimpered and arched into him.

She would have sworn she heard a chuckle. But her tongue was otherwise engaged, so a tongue-lashing would have to wait until later. He fumbled for something to the left, and the elevator came to an abrupt halt.

He skimmed his thumb over her breast, and a spike of desire rolled through her, causing her to undulate her hips. With a muffled moan, Tristan scooped a hand over her ass and held her tighter to him, pressing his erection into her.

His tongue slid over hers and he sucked her tongue into his mouth, making her want him, making her need him, making her wet.

Tristan tore his lips from hers and dragged in ragged breaths. Syn forced her eyes open and met his blistering gaze. When he spoke, his voice was low. Gravelly. "Now's a good time to stop me if you don't want to do this."

What? It took three tries to process the words that came out of his mouth.

"I— What?"

"Do you want this? Do you want me?"

She fought her heavy lids. The word *no* didn't even enter into her mind. "Yes."

A long exhale tore from his chest and he muttered something that sounded like "Thank God."

Tristan loved everything about the way she tasted. Spicy, with just a hint of sweet. He'd been slowly losing his mind as he watched that guy hit on her. He wanted to be the one she laughed with. And now she was in his arms and she wanted *him.*

He looped her hands over her head and clamped them in place with one hand. With his other hand, he hitched up her dress, slowly and deliberately.

Her lips parted on a sigh and she relaxed her thighs, slightly opening her legs for him. His cock throbbed.

A tremor ran through her body and he kissed her softly, still sliding his hand up her dress. At the juncture of her thighs, Tristan dragged the back of his knuckles over her panties and she pulled in a shuddering breath. "You're so responsive. I bet you're soft as butter too, aren't you?"

She mumbled something unintelligible and Tristan swallowed hard. His hand shook as his fingers traced the edge of her panty line. He watched her face intently for a hint of hesitation, but there was none. Only the same longing need that drove him.

He slid his finger just under the fabric and she dug her nails into the flesh of his hand. Her legs widened and he held his breath. So damn wet. So hot.

His found her slick entrance and slid the tip of his finger inside her. Syn tossed her head back and bit her lip. God, he might come just from watching her, she was so beautiful. As he slid in farther, he bit back a curse. "You're so tight."

"Tristan, please."

He kissed her again, sliding his finger in deeper as he did. While he sucked on her tongue in time to his questing finger, he slid his thumb over her clit.

She bucked and tore her lips from his. "Oh, oh, oh."

With another gentle stroke of his thumb, she flew apart in his arms, whispering his name.

Chapter 6

Shudders racked Syn's body. Tristan Dawson had just made her come. And she wanted more. *Needed* more. She slid her tongue over his and rolled her hips into his hand.

He released her hands and shrugged off his jacket before digging out his wallet. Reaching for him, with frantic, trembling fingers, Syn slipped his belt from its loop and he growled low.

She watched him intently as she slid her hand inside his trousers. When she closed her palm around the scorching hot length of him, he dropped his forehead to hers and cursed. She let her hand slide to the tip and smoothed the drop of precome over the head of his erection. She squeezed him gently as she slid her hand to the root and he swayed into her, his hips bucking slightly.

"Wow, Syn…" His voice trailed and his breathing was heavy and labored. "Do you have any idea how close I am to losing it?"

Oh boy. She could do this to him? The feminine power went to her head and she slid her palm over him again. *This* was why Tristan Dawson was so dangerous. His ability to make a woman believe she was sexy and powerful and a goddess.

He snagged a hand around her wrist. Her gaze snapped to his. He pierced her soul with the naked lust and need and...longing she saw there.

Tristan kissed her again, and her insides turned to liquid. He slid her hand from his flesh and quickly shrugged out of his pants. He yanked a condom out of his wallet and sheathed himself with a quick efficiency that she marveled at.

When he turned his attention back to her, she quivered. To be the object of that kind of focus was overwhelming. He slid his hands under her dress again, his gaze on hers as he took hold of the silk, then ripped.

Syn sucked in a sharp breath as the fabric ripped off her skin. Tristan kissed up her body. When he reached her lips, his thumbs stroked over her cheeks as he kissed her. A move so tender in contrast with the way he'd devoured her mouth like a starving man.

Tristan lifted her again and Syn willingly wrapped her legs around him. Syn arched her back and he leaned forward, nuzzling one breast, before suckling the tip. He palmed the other and tested the weight while teasing the nipple.

Syn arched into his palm, spreading her legs wider to make room for him between her thighs. Gently he teased her nipple, sending a spear of need through her core. "Tristan."

He positioned himself at her slick center. "Look at me," he whispered.

Syn disobeyed and let her eyelids flutter closed.

He chuckled and rolled his thumb over her nipple. The moment she arched her back, looking for more, he ceased the action. "I said, look at me."

She dragged her eyes open. "Stop teasing me."

His lips tipped into a smile. "I want to see your eyes when I sink into you."

Inch by inch he slid into her, both of them holding their breaths. Syn grasped on to his shoulders, digging into his flesh for support, while Tristan slid his hands under her ass, cupping her as he sank deep into her.

It was all too much. All too intimate. She tried to look away. But with every shift, he met her gaze. There was no hiding the intimacy between them. No running from it. No hiding from the vulnerability.

The thick length of him rocked inside her, then retreated slowly. The tension coiled deep inside her as she slid her hands into his hair. As he nuzzled into her neck, she tugged on his hair slightly and he hissed, "Harder."

He complied and his big body shuddered. He nipped at her jaw, then her collarbone.

He stroked deeper, each deep thrust hitting both her clit and that hidden spot deep inside.

"Oh my goodness," she whispered.

"God, you're beautiful…so long…wanted you."

With whispered sex words muttered in the darkness, the shiver of bliss came on strong, snaking rapidly down her spine. The spasming racking her whole body and ending in her toes. But it wasn't until he lifted his head and kissed her deep and slid a hand between them to stroke the bundle of nerves between her folds that she flew apart, unable to hold on to her illusion of control any longer.

"You're so sexy when you come." With another deep stroke, Tristan groaned into her neck, his whole body shuddering.

Chapter 7

Syn woke surrounded by warmth. As she snuggled
deeper into the covers, she smiled contentedly. Wow,
she hadn't slept that well in…well, hell, she couldn't remember ever sleeping that well. Raising her hands above
her head, she stretched, relieving aching muscles from
the tips of her fingers to the tippy top of her manicured
toes. As she wiggled back in toward her heat source, she
let her eyes drift shut again and as usual her brain took
her to her favorite fantasy. *Tristan.*

The scruff of his jaw tickling her inner thighs as he
lapped at her slick folds, giving her orgasm after orgasm,
unrelenting even when she begged off. Tristan, gently
placing her hands on the headboard, then bracketing her
hips in his big, strong hands as he took her from behind.
Tristan, begging her to say his name, insisting she admit
to who was inside, taking her to the blissful edge time
after time.

Tristan, who kissed her and told her she was beautiful and stared at her in awe as she came. Tristan, who worshipped her breasts and her ass. *Tristan. Tristan. Tristan.*

Except, this dream was different. As she played her fantasies over and over in her mind as it was her favorite in-desperate-need-of therapy pastime, her core tightened. That wasn't unusual, but the mild soreness was. But she wasn't sore in a bad way. More as though she'd had sex so good you want to slap your ex. As though she'd had sex so good it required an encore. As though she'd had sex so good she needed to give Tristan Dawson a freaking medal.

Her eyes sprang open. Carefully she peeked out of the corner of her eyes. Sure enough, Tristan lay beside her in all his gorgeous glory, looking devastatingly sexy and at the same time somehow vulnerable while he slept.

Shiiiiite. Her whole body seized as the memories flooded her brain. She'd slept with Tristan. More like that they'd screwed each other senseless and promptly passed out. She was officially *that* girl. The girl who couldn't control her freaking hormones. The girl she'd made fun of. She'd been *Dawsoned*.

She'd slept with the enemy. Not only slept with him; she'd lost count of the number of orgasms he'd given her. But what she hadn't lost track of was the way he looked at her every time he slid into her. As if he was in awe and she felt like Christmas morning. And she'd seen that look at least five times during the night. The man was a sex god. She really had to find out what kind of vitamins he took.

And damned if he didn't believe in ladies *first*…and ladies *second*…sometimes even ladies *third* before he came. After each time when she passed out, they'd slept for about an hour, and then he'd woken her up again for

more of his expert tongue and hands. Each time she'd
gone willingly and given as good as she'd gotten. The
floodgates of sexual tension were now released.

Okay, calm down, Syn. First order of business, wake
that sexy man up for round five. *No!* She was not going
to have sex with him…*again.* Her libido was not running
the show. *Yes, I am.* She ignored the roaring diva inside
and forced her brain out of autopilot, revving the engine.
The real first order of business was to get the hell out
of bed. She'd be able to think better when his warmth
didn't envelop her like a cocoon. Second order of business, find her dress.

She risked another glance at him before she quietly slid
to the edge of the bed. In the darkness of the room, she
used her foot to search for it. He'd tossed it on the floor
somewhere here, right? Their first time had been so hurried in the elevator. Still inside her, he'd carried her into
his bedroom before cleaning them both up. He'd tossed
her dress somewhere on the floor during round two. She'd
been so shell-shocked and lust-crazed she hadn't paid attention to where he'd dropped it.

Behind her, Tristan shifted in the bed, and she froze.
First rule of one-night stand with a sex god: don't stick
around for the awful morning after with said sex god.
Second rule of one-night stand with a sex god: don't have
the sex god be Tristan Dawson. Third rule of one-night
stand with a sex god…do it again and burn the memories into your brain. Syn bit back a moan. *Stupid move,
Michaels.* If she thought he was impossible before, there
would be no getting that smug look off his face now.

Where the hell was her dress? *Screw it, you can buy
another one.*

Right now, in the darkness of Tristan's room with her
heart hammering, and her lady parts begging for more

of what Tristan had to offer, the best course of action was to cut and run. Staying here was too dangerous. But without her dress, that meant walking out of his room butt naked. There would be no sexy movie scene where she slid out of bed with a sheet covering her lady parts. This was real life and if she grabbed a sheet, that would certainly wake him.

Come on, once more with feeling. Get up and get gone. Once in the comfort of her room, she could figure out how to get the ground to open and swallow her whole. One thing was for certain, she'd have to check in to another hotel and do the rest of her observations as a third party. It was the only way.

As she stood, a voice from behind her said, "Running away, Michaels?"

She squeaked and whirled around. Damn him for looking so hot. Yes, she was running away, but she wasn't going to let him know that. "No. Going back to my room. We have an early morning, so I need to get some sleep. I can't do that here."

He reached over and turned on the light on the nightstand. Synthia dived for the sheets, but only managed to grab enough to cover her breasts to about the top of her thighs. *Well, hell.* But at least if they were going to have this conversation, he couldn't ogle her boobs. Too bad her butt was flapping in the wind.

Tristan reached for her and Synthia backed up a step. Unfortunately it also shifted the sheet, so she nearly flashed him her vajayjay. No matter that he had already seen her goods up close and personal. In her version of the awkward morning after, she'd be clad in designer chic with perfect makeup and styled hair. Instead, her hair was a tangled sweaty rat's nest, and her makeup was likely smeared all over her face and she was bare-assed naked, trying to make a clean escape. *So* not perfect. She cleared her throat. "I'm going back to my room, Tristan."

He frowned and shoved himself into a sitting position. "Why?"

"Because, I need sleep and you, we, um—last night. I—" Okay, so maybe next time she opened her mouth, she'd use actual words. Intelligent words. Rational words. But right now the more she searched, the more she came up empty, or naked, as it would seem.

Even in the muted morning light, his gaze pierced her straight to the soul. "The way I figure it, you can run back to your room and you can pretend that last night in the elevator, and in the doorway, and in this bed, and the middle of the night when I woke you up to finally see how you taste, or an hour ago when I slid into you from behind, holding those perfect boobs of yours, didn't happen. Or you can come back to bed and we can call some kind of truce."

A truce. He wanted a truce with her? "Look, I don't ever do..." Her voice trailed off and she gestured vaguely with her hand. "That. I'm cautious and I don't sleep around."

He sighed and scrubbed his hands over his beautiful face. "Syn, I didn't plan last night."

Irritation flared. Why wouldn't he just let her go? "Ya think?"

He turned a narrowed gaze in her direction, and her core clenched. How the hell did she want him again? His effect on women was an unfair advantage. And with the ache between her thighs, she was weak.

"What I was saying is, I might not have planned it, but I'm not sorry it happened."

Of course *he* wasn't. He'd added a notch to his belt. He'd officially thrown her off her game and he wanted to gloat and relish in it. He continued. "You and I, obviously, the chemistry is out of this world."

She shifted uncomfortably. But yeah, he had a point.

"And in bed, we work." He nodded as he studied the disarray of the bed. "Obviously, as evidenced last night, now that I've touched you, it's become something of an addiction."

She tugged harder on the sheet, willing more to give way so she could cover her butt too. "What are you saying, Tristan?"

He sighed. "I don't want to be your enemy for the next two days. And I don't want to be your enemy in the office. I never wanted that. I want to call a truce."

What? Was he insane? "I want to make sure I'm hearing this right."

"I'm saying why don't you come back to bed and maybe you'll let me kiss all your birthmarks again and then we'll wake up and have breakfast?"

She blinked. Oh, okay, he wanted to live in a pretend world. In a world where she hadn't just screwed her biggest competition. *In a world where you had the best sex of your life.* She shook off the thought. "Tristan, we can't just pretend that we're on a lovers' weekend."

"For two days, we can. Maybe we could pretend we weren't on opposite sides and we weren't fighting for the same gig and, shocker of shocker, we could pretend we actually liked each other. I'd rather spend the next two nights with you in my bed, making love to you, than lying in an empty bed pretending I'm not thinking about you."

"Tristan, we need to use our heads. We leave on Monday. What happens when we go back to work?"

"We go back to normal. And maybe we find some common ground. Maybe we act like we don't hate each other."

He made it sound so easy, but it wasn't. "If this gets around at the office, only your career stays intact. Nobody would take me seriously anymore."

He shook his head. "But I wouldn't do that. What happens here stays here. This *is* Vegas, after all."

Could she do that? Just enjoy him for enjoyment's sake? *Yes,* her inner sex goddess shouted. But one thing eluded her. "Why?"

He slid his gaze from hers. "I know that you think I'm a womanizing jerk, but that's not who I am."

"So what is the truth?"

He shrugged. "Most people, women especially, see what I look like, they hear the Dawson name, and that's all it takes. I'm not going to lie and say I didn't reap the benefits of those things before. But they're not all I am. I'm more than my name. I work hard to prove that."

Synthia quirked an eyebrow. "So what you're saying is you don't want to be objectified for your body."

His smirk was rueful. "Well, let's not get carried away. If you're the one doing the objectifying, then I think I'm down for that."

She rolled her eyes. "Of course you are."

His eyes softened. "Syn, you intrigue me. From the moment I saw you, you've been under my skin. You surprise me. You're smart and I find it sexy. And hands down, there is no one else I'd rather fight with. You make me bring my A-game. And last night wasn't nearly enough." He reached his hand out for her again.

She thought what to do was say to hell with the sheet and head back to her room, giving him a bird's-eye view of her ass. What she should do was tell him to take his charm and his designed-to-make-a-woman-crumble words and feed those lines to someone dumb enough to believe him. What she should do was tell him to forget this ever happened.

Should, should, should. But if she was honest with herself, she'd admit she wanted more of that intimacy. She wanted more of that chance to be carefree. She wanted more of that intense tenderness. She wanted to feel as if she were the only woman in the world again. Even if it was short-lived. Even if it wasn't real. She wanted to live in a pretend world where she didn't have to be perfect. Where she could breathe and relax. Where she could just feel.

She licked her lips. "We go back to normal on Monday?"

He nodded. "No one will know but us. I swear it."

Synthia shifted on her feet again. "And for the rest of the weekend we're calling a truce?"

His lips turned up at the corners, and her belly flipped. "I, for one, enjoyed the angry sex, but I prefer not fighting with you in bed or otherwise. We still do our jobs, clearly, but no reason we can't work together."

There was sincerity in his eyes and she wanted to believe. She glanced at his still-outstretched hand and for the first time in her adult life, she did the unplanned thing and took a leap.

Chapter 8

"You're not afraid of heights, are you?" Tristan asked as they buckled themselves into the helicopter early the next morning. The excursion at breathtaking heights was part of the hotel's VIP package.

Syn slid him a withering glance even while her hands shook a little. "I'm good," she shouted over the roar of the propellers.

He laughed. She was stubborn, even when it was in her best interest not to be. "You know, we don't have to do this. We can pick something tamer."

"Are you going through with this?"

He grinned. "Of course. A chance to see the Grand Canyon from above? Hell yes."

She gave him a fragile smile. "Then yes, I need to do this."

Tristan shook his head. "Are you always this competitive?"

She grinned and he was momentarily stunned. "You should see me play cards."

"Remind me never to play poker with you."

She patted his knee. "Not if you like to keep your money. My dad taught me to play to win, every time."

His gaze fixed on her hand, and his sex-dulled brain cells begged for her to go higher up his thigh. *Damn*. He needed to get this under control. After he'd coaxed her back to bed, they made love…twice. And to be ever so helpful, his brain replayed the reel of her riding him, taking him deep. He blinked several times, trying to change the image. The one he got as a replacement wasn't much better. Him, between her legs, making her come until she screamed his name. Yeah. Any minute now, he'd work her out of his system. *Liar*.

But even more than the sex, he liked her. When she wasn't busy trying to complicate his life, she was pretty funny and he enjoyed talking to her. He searched for a safer topic of conversation. "Is your dad hard on you?"

"He was tough. But fair. He believed that I could win at anything as long as I fought hard enough. Sometimes I'm not the most gracious loser."

He cocked his head and laughed. "I guess it doesn't matter if you usually win."

She chuckled and shifted her gaze out of the window. "Yeah, but when interlopers come in and give me a run for my money, I'm perhaps less than forgiving."

He blinked and raised his eyebrows. "Oh no, is this one of those rare Syn Michaels apologies? In the two years since I started at Stellar Reach, I don't think I've ever heard you say you're sorry."

"Don't get used to it. But I've been hard on you. Some of it deserved, but some of it, I was testing you for being the new guy."

He shrugged. "Maybe I was a bit of a jerk too. I saw Bill Meyers at a bar the night before your presentation and seized the opportunity to make my pitch. I had a jump start."

Her jaw dropped. "I knew it. I knew it." She smacked his arm. "I couldn't even get him to pay a lick of attention to me."

"Wow. You're surprisingly strong." He clasped her hands in between his. "Would you relax? I'm saying I'm sorry."

"You had me thinking I'd lost my mind."

"I know." Wisely he changed the subject before she could decide that she hated him again. "So, is your old man proud of you now? You're making a name for yourself. Your competitive nature helped you get there."

A shadow passed over her face, and her grin dropped into a slight smile. "I hope he would have been."

He frowned, not understanding.

She continued more quietly. "My parents died seven years ago when I was seventeen."

Damn. "I'm so sorry. I had no idea. That must have been really hard."

Her voice was soft. "Yeah, it was. But we Michaels women are tough. My uncle took us in for a couple of years after. The moment I started school and started interning, my sister and I moved to our own place." She shrugged. "We've been looking out for each other ever since."

Wow, at twenty-four, she'd already experienced so much loss and accomplished so much. He was a year older and he still felt as though he was foundering. Unsure of what to say to her, he reached out and took her hand. "I'm sure they would have been really proud of you."

She quickly changed the subject. "So I guess this is old hat to you. You probably grew up with your own helipad."

He laughed. "No, actually. I've never been on a helicopter. My brother is the adventurer. You name some death-defying act and he's probably done it. He's the one who gave me some ideas of what to test out here in Vegas. Growing up, I was the one who was focused on the future. Sure, I got in a little trouble. But somehow I never saw the appeal of risking my life for kicks."

Her eyebrows rose. "Seriously? That ruins the whole playboy image I had of you."

He shrugged. "Sorry to disappoint."

The helicopter lifted then and for the next hour, he held her hand. To his surprise, she let him. To his own surprise, he wanted to keep doing it. Throughout their tour, she'd squeeze his hand during banks and dips, and he'd squeeze back as a silent way of telling her it was okay. Her breath caught as the morning sunlight slashed over the enormous, jagged rock formations and sheer rock faces, bathing them in orange and yellow light and casting deep, russet shadows on the valleys below.

When they landed, she beamed a grin at him. "Okay, that was totally scary, but so awesome."

"Uh-oh, don't tell me I have a little adrenaline junkie on my hands. I've created a monster. I'll need to introduce you to my brother. The stories he could tell you about all the ways he's nearly killed himself would curl your toes."

"Easy, now. I like adrenaline as much as the next girl. I'm just not so keen on the heights thing. Or more like the I-can-fall-out-of-this-tin-can thing."

"You were perfectly safe up there with me. Or so I've been told."

She gave him a characteristic Syn smirk, and his dick twitched. "Said the spider to the fly."

"Does this spider look hungry?"

Immediately, her pupils dilated and her breath hitched. Man, he could get used to that hungry look on her face. He didn't need anything else in the world in that moment.

She leaned away from him and shook her head. "You're dangerous."

"Same could be said about you." He forced himself to take a deliberate step back. "Are you ready for our next adventure?"

"Let me guess, you want to throw me from a building and see if I can fly?"

"Not today. Besides, I didn't see any wings on that beautiful back of yours, so that kind of adventure would ruin plans I have for you over the next two nights. Guess again."

Syn shrugged. "Surprise me."

"I didn't think you were much for surprises, but okay." They stepped out of the helicopter and rounded the back of the helipad and on the other side waiting were a Bugatti Veyron and a Pagani Huayra.

Her eyes went round and she squeaked as she spoke. "Is that a Bugatti?"

"You know cars?"

"Hello, avid *Top Gear* fan. The UK version, not that watered-down American version they show here." Even though she vibrated with energy, she hesitated.

"What's the matter? Neither of these something you like? And here I thought you were an adrenaline queen." She laughed and he relished the sound of it.

"Ease up, Silver Spoon. I'm just trying to determine if I want style or speed."

He leaned forward and the hint of her strawberry shampoo wreaked havoc with his senses. "Here's a hint, honey. They're both fast. They are race cars, after all."

She raised an eyebrow. "Yes, but you and I both know which one is faster hands down and I'm trying to decide if kicking your butt is more important, or if looking oh so pretty while I do it will be better."

Kicking his— The laugh bubbled up from somewhere deep inside him. While her competitiveness usually drove him nuts, right now it made him desperate to kiss her.

Tristan looped his arms around her waist and pulled her in quick. Her lips parted on a gasp and he took full advantage.

So maybe kissing her wasn't his best idea if he wanted to think clearly, but he needed to touch her. As his lips molded to hers, she tentatively wound her hands around his neck. She tasted so good. And she fit so perfectly against him.

His erection twitched against her belly, and a little mewling sound escaped the back of her throat, driving him crazy. All he wanted to do was drag her back into that helicopter and sink deep into her. He licked into her mouth, tasting, sipping and savoring, unable to get enough. A sudden thought filtered into his mind. They had an audience. With a frustrated growl, he tore his lips from hers. Dragging in ragged breaths, he squeezed her briefly before letting go. "It seems I have a problem controlling myself with you."

Synthia brushed her fingers over her lips. "You should come with a hazardous-to-brain-cells warning label."

"So, what's it going to be? You going to stay true to form or you going to give me a chance at winning our little race here?"

She smirked. "What do you think? I choose making you eat my dust."

Tristan shook his head. "Should have known. Not to

worry. I don't need the faster car. I'm a good driver, so I'm still in this race."

"Do you have an unfair advantage here?"

He grinned. "I'm a virgin, honey." He winked when she barked out a laugh. "A race car virgin. I just believe in myself."

She laughed as she donned a helmet and slid behind the wheel of the car. He mimicked her actions. There was no way he was betting her, but man, he loved to see her competitive juices flowing. It made her eyes sparkle, and that smart mouth of hers gave him ideas. An image flashed in his mind of her putting that smart mouth to use all over his body, and he groaned. Advantage Syn.

"You have to admit I came close," Tristan said once they were settled comfortably in the limousine.

Laughter bubbled up inside Synthia. "In what universe? I beat you by a hundred yards." Her blood hummed through her body, and electricity coursed through her veins. She loved this feeling. She looked forward to every casual touch. It was as if once her body knew what it was missing, it wanted it all the time. How was she ever going to survive this? *Stop. Monday is a long way away.*

"Penny for your thoughts?"

There was no way she would tell him what she was actually thinking about. "Nothing. Just going over my spectacular win again in my head."

He shook his head and tucked a finger under her chin, turning her to face him. "Don't hide from me. That wasn't excitement, or happiness or even smugness on your face. It was irritation. What's up?"

She pulled her chin from his grip. "Nothing. I swear."

"C'mon, be honest with me. This is Vegas, remember? It stays here."

Synthia bit her lip. "I'm just readjusting some initial thoughts about you, is all. I pictured you more as the lounging-in-a-hot-tub-surrounded-by-women kind of guy."

His gaze was intent on her face and he clamped his jaw tight. "Wow. Such a high opinion of me." He sighed. "As a general rule of thumb, I only deal with one woman at a time, whether it's for a weekend or it's for a year."

Now she wished she'd kept that to herself. "I guess I'm surprised."

"About what?"

"Well, I know your reputation. The women in the office talk about you all the time. I guess I had you figured wrong."

He chuckled mirthlessly. "It's not exactly like I steered you away from that impression."

She raised an eyebrow. "So you're not some international playboy?"

He smiled. "An international playboy, huh? I guess I do have quite the reputation."

"What? You're telling me it's not true?" Could she believe that? She'd seen him flirting with everything in a skirt.

"Look, I like women. All kinds of women." He shrugged. "And I'm a bit of a flirt. But I don't sleep with every women who flirts with me, nor do I want to. Like I said, I like to keep it simple. One at a time. Besides, so many women I meet want to go out with *Tristan Dawson*, and not just Tristan."

She frowned. She'd never given it much thought before. But there was a lot of muttering about Cinderella fantasies when he'd started. "I suppose you never really know if someone likes you for you or for the Dawson name."

"Rich boy problems, right?"

"Kind of," she said with a shrug.

He laughed. "One thing I always know with you. You are honest. It didn't matter to you who I was when I started. All you ever cared about was if I was any good at my job."

She flushed and cringed. "Not entirely true. I heard you were a Dawson and I had my preconceived notions about who you would be. I suppose I make my fair share of Silver Spoon, Richie Rich and Junior Warbucks jokes."

His laugh was rich and low. "True. But that's you giving me a hard time. Besides, with you, my family name is more something to overcome. Since I was old enough to know what my father did or the fact that we weren't like other kids in the world, I was sort of already disillusioned with the money. Dad used to say things like 'This is not how I expect a Dawson to act.' Or 'Tristan, you're a Dawson. You should know better.' I always felt like it was more about the disgrace I'd bring to the name than me. If he'd just changed it and said 'This is not how I expect *you* to act,' life would have been a whole different story."

"I take it the two of you don't get along?"

"Yeah, you could say that. He pretty much disowned me when I said I wasn't going into the family business."

Her heart squeezed. Growing up, she would have been jealous of someone like Tristan, having both parents and more money than Midas, but it seemed he'd faced his share of problems, as well. "I'm sorry, I didn't know."

He shrugged. "I see my mom about once a month, but Dad and I don't speak, unless he's calling to try to force me into working for him. To him, I'm a loser and waste of talent."

A heavy silence filled the air for several moments. Then she spoke. "You're not a loser. You're doing things on your own terms. He might not like it, but he has to respect it on some level."

"Yeah, well, try telling *him* that."

"No offense, but your father's a bit of a jerk."

His characteristic grin was back in place. "Funny, I've told him the same thing before."

The limousine pulled up to the hotel and she stifled the regret. They were here to work, after all, and she still had to check out the facilities. It didn't matter that she'd rather spend the rest of the afternoon finding out more about him. *Check yourself, Syn. This isn't real.* Whatever happened tonight, she had to remind herself of that; otherwise she would get hurt.

Chapter 9

Tristan had spent the past hour checking out the private betting rooms. He was even up a little, considering he'd been playing some high stakes. The perfect kind of gambling—here he didn't have to assume any of the risk. As part of the VIP package, Bella had provided gambling money. After all, he had to look the part.

When he opened the door to the suite, it smelled fantastic. "Wow, you cook?"

Syn's smile was bright and sunny. "Hey."

He grinned. "Hey, yourself. You look happy."

"Well, I figured we could have a late lunch. I had this fantastic kitchen and I wanted to test it out at least once."

He laughed. "Yeah, me too. But somehow I think we have different ideas about the definition of try it out."

She laughed and shook her head. "You're incorrigible."

"And sexy. Don't forget sexy." As automatically as if he'd been doing it for cameras, he swung an arm around her and twirled her into a dance. "One thing I want to make a habit."

She scrunched her nose. "Oh yeah, what's that?"

"This." He kissed her deeply. No preamble, no lead-up. Just fused their mouths together and tried to sate some of the hunger for her.

When he released her, she blinked sleepily. "Okay, you should always do that when you see me."

"Done. Though it could make for the weird and awkwards around the office." Her smile faltered and he realized what he'd said. *Damn it.*

She recovered quicker than he did. "You'd miss me calling you Silver Spoon too much."

"I think of it as a term of endearment." He swatted her on the butt. "So, what's making my mouth water?"

"I hope you like Cuban. I made this shrimp and rice dish I had at Cubana Libre in Miami. I harassed the chef via email for ten months before he'd give the goods on his recipe."

"Somehow I can totally see you doing that."

She shrugged her slim shoulders. "So I'm a little persistent. Nothing wrong with that."

"Not a thing. It's probably why I like you."

She quirked an eyebrow. "You mean it's not my ass?"

Tristan laughed. "Okay, admittedly, that might have a little to do with it. But if we're being serious, it's your snarky and persistent attitude, then your laugh, *then* your ass."

"Wow, that ass ranks third, huh? I have to say I'm surprised."

"Oh, really? And what is it you like about me?"

She stirred something on the stove, and her smile turned serious. "That you surprise me. Just when I think I have you figured out, you switch it up again. It keeps me guessing. Those eyes of yours don't hurt either. And, well, your abs. I hope you don't mind, but I plan on doing a load of laundry on them later."

"As long as you do the load naked, I'm not really bothered." He took a position on one of the stools at the island. "Do you cook for your sister a lot?"

"Not so much anymore now that she doesn't live with me. She has her own place close to campus. The only time she comes home to my place now is to do laundry or to go grocery shopping."

He frowned. "Grocery shopping, not my thing."

Syn hitched a thumb and pointed at the fridge. "No worries, we're well stocked."

"You know you didn't have to cook. We're in Vegas with world-class restaurants on every corner."

Syn shrugged. "I don't get to cook much for people, and cooking for one is so dull. I made more of an effort to be home for family dinner when Xia lived with me, but I guess little sister had to grow up sometime."

"I hear they do that."

"You know, I don't even know if you have siblings."

"I have a brother, Taylor, and a sister, Tawny."

"Oh, the T names. You were *that* family."

He coughed out a laugh. "Yes, my mother's name is Trista, so you can imagine how my name came about. Then it was a tradition, so…"

Syn clutched a hand to her chest as she laughed. "I am so sorry."

"Yeah, me too." Man, she was so pretty. Putzing around the kitchen in her bare feet and apron was not something he ever pictured her doing. It seemed she could surprise him too. "So, how long till lunch?"

"About twenty minutes. Give or take. Would you like me to make you a drink?"

"Wow, that is very fifties housewife of you."

She laughed and tossed a towel at his head. "Don't go getting used to this. I expect you to be a cabana boy, peeling my grapes later."

He waggled his eyebrows. "Is that a euphemism? 'Cause, done deal. So how about I steal my kisses now since after lunch we should do some work."

"I might not be opposed to that."

Tristan stalked over to her with a grin and she backed up. He kissed her deep, loving every moment of being with her. Picking her up, he sat her on the counter, stepping between her legs. It wasn't long before he was sliding his hands under her blouse and she was dragging his shirt off his back.

What was it about this woman that always made him lose complete control of the situation?

"Tristan."

Mmm, the way she said his name made him hard. "Yeah, baby?" She tasted like sweet and spice and he slid a hand between the two of them. Through the denim of her jeans, he stroked his thumb over her sex. And she bowed into him.

"I need—"

A sharp ringing sound broke through the sexual fog.

She tore her lips from his. "Damn, that's my sister Xia's ringtone. I need to get that."

Even though sexual frustration clawed at him, he dragged on his T-shirt and then gently set Syn back on the floor. "We're going to pick this up later."

"Promises, promises," she muttered.

He tried to give her a bit of privacy for her call, but he couldn't help overhearing Syn's part of the conversation. "Yeah…relax, I know it's due…working on it…

ever let you down before…I'll make it happen. You will graduate, I promise."

She was paying for her sister's tuition? Concern for her burned in his gut. She had been serious about looking after her little sister. While for him, his job was about getting ahead and earning respect, for her, it was about survival.

Chapter 10

After lunch, Tristan spent a few hours checking out the gym and talking to the trainers. When he returned to the suite, he dressed quickly for dinner. Tonight the plan was dinner followed up by a concert by pop star Coco Goldstein, who the hotel had booked for a two-year Vegas residence. Tickets had sold out within forty-five minutes of going on sale. Too bad a crowded concert venue was the last place he wanted to be with Syn. What he wanted to do was stay in with her, and enjoy her body. Especially if he wasn't going to get to touch her again after Sunday.

The thought of going back to LA had him clenching his teeth. He wasn't going to think about it. He'd focus on now. When he could touch her, when he could keep them locked in here making love for hours. They could blow off tonight. If you'd seen one concert, you'd seen them all, right? And bumping and grinding with Syn's sweet ass pressed into his lap was a recipe for torture and a public indecency citation.

He knocked on her door. "Hey, so before you get dressed—"

The door to her bedroom swung open and he stared. Her makeup was darker than usual, dramatic. He liked her normally natural look, but this was pretty too. She looked the part of a vamped-up sex goddess. The ruby-red lipstick beckoned to him to kiss it off.

She twirled around and his dick throbbed. Where was the rest of that dress? Last night's number had been backless. This one was dangerously short. As though, if she shifted the wrong way, the world would get too much of a private view.

He swallowed hard, unable to find words. Instead several scenarios went through his head. All of them involved her with no panties. He studied the dress again. Dare he hope? Was there enough of a thrill seeker inside her to go commando? Would she let him find out?

"Yo, earth to Tristan, did you hear me?" She snapped fingers in front of his eyes.

He blinked, then focused on her beautiful face. "Huh?"

"I asked what you were trying to ask me?"

Ask her? Yes, there had been something he wanted to know. Too bad he couldn't remember it now. He stalked into her bedroom.

She backed up. "Oh no, you don't. I know that look."

He took another step forward and she retreated. "What look?"

"The look that says you're dying to do something we don't have time for."

"We can be late."

Syn shook her head. "Tristan. We're supposed to be working, remember?"

Work. Right. That thing he was in Vegas to do. "You're right. But I have plans for you later."

She cocked her head. "Who says *I* don't have plans for *you*?" Her red lips parted slightly, and she dropped her voice to a whisper. "Have I mentioned I've been dying to taste you?"

Pleasure zinged down his spine and settled low in his belly. He burned for her. "See, I was prepared to be a good boy, but then you said that."

She gave a nervous laugh. "Tristan…dinner, remember?" She put both her hands up, but she giggled.

"Come here, Syn."

Her grin turned cheeky. "Make me."

She was quicker than he thought, but he still caught her and looped his arms around her waist. "See, when you make me chase you, there's going to be a punishment."

With every laugh and giggle, his chest warmed. God, she was pretty. And yes, of course, she was scorching hot and her body was unreal, but there was something soft and feminine and real about her smile. It always made him pause.

"You can punish me after dinner, because—" She stopped talking and something between a moan and a groan escaped her soft lips as he nuzzled her throat.

"What is that perfume? It's been driving me crazy since I met you. Sweet, but a hint of spice. When I'm near you it's all I can do not to lean in to get a better sniff." He kissed along the column of her throat and she whimpered. "Tristan."

"Mmm."

"You're dangerous."

"Oh, I know."

He trailed kisses up her neck and jawline, finally landing one on her lips. She parted them on a sigh and delved in. The kiss turned from exploratory to sizzling hot in less than three seconds. Next thing he knew, he was desperate to get as close to her as he could. He wanted to shut out the outside world and lose himself in the woman.

When she slipped her hands into his hair, he deepened the kiss. Feeling her nails scoring his scalp drove him nuts, and she knew it.

He slid one hand up her thigh, teasing the flesh just at the hem. Syn hummed into his mouth and he took that as acceptance. Slipping his hand underneath the gossamer sliver of fabric, he paused just short of the juncture at her thighs.

Syn whimpered again and he dragged his lips from hers. "Do you want to go? Or do you want to stay here with me?"

She arched her body into him and tugged on his hair again. "That's not playing fair."

"Who said anything about fair?" He laughed. "The way I figure it, you've been torturing me for two years. You have all kinds of payback coming your way."

"Well, if you hadn't acted like such a moron for two years, we could have been doing this a lot sooner."

He met her gaze. Did she mean that? Could there have been something between them outside of this moment in time? Beyond Sin City, where they could be irresponsible and not think about the future? He shoved the thought aside. *Focus on the now. Focus on the fun.* "You might have a point there." He slid the back of his knuckles over her sex, and they both froze.

"Is there something you want to tell me, Synthia?"

She shivered. "What? You mean about the no under-wear thing? That was supposed to be a surprise for later, but you're pretty freaking impatient."

Man, he was keeping this woman. *Forever.* He

frowned. Where had that thought come from? Tristan cleared his throat as he slid a finger between her silky smooth lips. If he wasn't careful, he'd come right here. "Is there something else you want to tell me?"

She squirmed in his arms, trying to arch her body closer to his questing hand. She shook her head slightly and grinned. "Nope, nothing else really. Why, is there something you've noticed?"

Noticed? He was on the verge of orgasm and she wanted to tease him. Fine, he could play along, but he wasn't going to give her the upper hand here. "Well, I seem to remember some hair right here, yesterday." He slid his fingers over the delicate lips again, making sure she got his meaning. "Want to tell me what happened to it?"

Still giggling, she blinked her eyes rapidly. "I was mugged. It all happened so fast. There was this big woman named Olga in the spa downstairs and she took everything I had. Left me with nothing."

Wow, she was awesome. He nuzzled her neck again. "Was it something of value? Should I go down and have Olga arrested? Or was it something you won't miss and maybe I should thank Olga?"

Syn rotated her hips just so, bringing his finger in contact with her clit. "You can probably thank her. That is, if you like this sort of thing."

If he liked— Tristan bit off a curse. "Yeah, I like it."

"I certainly hope so, because you ruined my surprise."

"I promise, I'll make it up to you."

"Just how do you plan on doing that?" she breathed.

Tristan slid a finger into her slick moist depths, and at the same time rotated his thumb over her clit. What he wanted to do was bury his dick deep inside her and never move again, hopefully dying from pleasure.

But since he'd ruined her surprise, he decided to show restraint. He slid his finger from her, then brought it to his lips and licked it clean. "Have I told you how incredible you taste?"

She blinked up at him with wide, dark eyes. "No."

"Then by all means, let me show you." He told himself the kiss would be quick. That he wouldn't prolong it. He told himself he would hold her a little away from him before he lost control. But there was no taking things slow and easy with Syn. Every kiss felt as if he kissed a live wire. As if it might just be possible to die of ecstasy.

She kissed him back, pulling him to her. It was her tug on his belt that brought the control back. If she dragged off his belt, they were never leaving this room. Not tonight, not tomorrow. And certainly not on Monday when they were due back. He would spend the time exploring every single nook and cranny of her body. Then spend time rediscovering it all again.

He released her abruptly. With sex-hazed, droopy lids, she stared at him. "What's wrong?"

He tried to bring his breathing back to normal. "Besides you driving me to the edge of reason? Nothing." He straightened and shoved his hands into his pockets. "We have dinner plans. And you said I should practice restraint."

The moment it dawned on her that they wouldn't be having a quickie, she scowled. "You got me all worked up."

He loved the way her eyes sparked with anger. "It helps build the anticipation."

Syn crossed her arms over those beautiful breasts. "Fair enough. Just remember that payback is a bitch wielding killer stilettos."

* * *

Synthia shifted uncomfortably in her seat. As seduction masters went, Tristan Dawson was a natural. The way he moved, the way he smiled. Even the way he ate. He'd been eye-sexing her from across their dinner table for most of the night. The way he licked tiramisu off that dessert spoon made her think of other things he could do with his tongue. To be the focus of that intense gaze was enough to melt her into a puddle. It didn't help that every so often his gaze would slip from her eyes and flicker down to her breasts. And traitorous body that she had, her nipples would immediately pebble.

She hadn't figured out how to get him back yet, but she would. And she'd make him pay. She bit back a laugh as she imagined herself from the ten-thousand-foot view. Was this really her? Sexy and fun and free. Not worrying about what was next, what would happen tomorrow? She liked the feeling. And it certainly wasn't her to run around in a short dress with no panties on. There was something about him that dared her to be bold.

Maybe this was only for a few days, but she'd at least take part of that with her. A slice of pain stabbed her heart and she shook it off. She wasn't going to think about it. She could enjoy this time and let it go. It was the best thing for her. Because getting involved with Tristan was sure to get her hurt. And she so wasn't down for that. He was also the best kind if distraction. But she had to keep her eyes on the prize, she had a job to do. Xia was depending on her.

"A penny for your thoughts?" he asked. His voice was soft, coaxing. As if he knew what she was thinking about and wanted to lighten her dark mood.

"Oh, I'm just thinking about how to repay you for the little stunt at the hotel."

His sexy grin was back in a flash and he leaned forward. "Who knew you were so impatient and hot for my body?"

She considered tossing her wine in his face, but that would be a waste of perfectly good wine. Of course, if he was naked, she could sip it off the grooves of his abs. *Focus, Syn. Operation payback is in full effect.* "Who said anything about impatient? I can wait." She licked her lips slowly and deliberately, and then dropped her voice to a whisper. "I've just been dying to taste you and I hoped I'd get the chance, but you cut us off before I could even find out. I was really disappointed."

His eyes darkened to navy and he called the waiter over. "Check please." He turned his attention to her. "We're going back to the hotel. We can skip the concert."

"But I really wanted to go. I love Coco's music."

Tristan ran his hands through his hair. "You're killing me, Syn."

"What was that I said about payback?"

The waiter brought the check and Tristan paid it without even looking at it. Bliss would be footing the bill anyway, but Synthia still wondered what that would be like. To not even look at the cost of something and get it just because she wanted it.

With her current job, things were easier and she'd certainly breathe a sigh of relief once Xia was out of school. But truth be told, she'd always worry about money. At this point it was a habit.

Tristan quirked his brow as he stood. "You ready?"

She stood smoothly and gave him a beatific smile. "Oh, I'm ready all right."

The muscle in his jaw ticked. "You really mean to pay me back?"

"You better believe it."

Tristan watched her like a caged animal and she bit the inside of her mouth to keep from smirking. He'd taken up post on the opposite side of the limo and she tried desperately not to flash him. How in the world did these starlets do it? As they pulled away from the restaurant, Tristan continued to watch her intently. She tried using his words against him. "Penny for your thoughts, Tristan?"

"You know what my thoughts are. And they include not leaving the hotel from the time we get back tonight until the flight on Monday."

"Promises, promises."

That muscle in his jaw ticked again and he turned his attention to look outside the window.

She tugged at the short skirt of her dress again. If she wanted to do this, then she'd better get to it. They only had thirty minutes to the show, and the limousine would arrive shortly. Syn pressed the intercom on her right. "Hey, Jake, do you think you could take the long way?"

Their driver answered in the affirmative.

She shifted herself forward and pushed so she could lean over him. This had never been her. She enjoyed sex as much as the next girl, but she'd never taken control before.

She kissed Tristan's lips softly and he immediately wove his hands into her hair. If she let him, he'd take over and that wasn't what she wanted…yet. She pulled back and he let out a frustrated groan. That was until she slipped his belt loop from his buckle.

Tristan snapped a hand around her wrist. "Syn…" It was part question, part plea. She ignored his staying hand and pulled down the zipper of his pin-striped pants, all the while not taking her gaze off his. "Yes, Tristan?"

"What are you doing?"

"Oh, you know, something I've been curious about for

a while now." She slid a hand inside his pants, and his lids fluttered closed with a groan.

When she released the full, hard length of him from his boxers, she rubbed the smooth tip with her thumb. A faint drop of moisture escaped the head and he hissed, his hips bucking upward. "Oh, Syn." Again, there was that hint of pleading.

When she wrapped her lips around him, he cursed and dug his hands into her hair. At first she wasn't sure if he was holding her in place or if he was pulling her off, but she didn't release him.

As she sucked him deep into her mouth, her hand slid down his shaft in a steady pace.

His skin was soft and hot and with every lick and slide, he coupled whispers of her name with dirty words of what he wanted her to do and how tight he wanted her grip, directing her. She was a more than capable student. She wanted him, wanted this. If she was going to walk away from this, she wanted everything with him for this slice of time.

His hand twitched and he held her still. She frowned and licked up the thick length of him again.

"Damn, it, Syn, if you don't stop, I'm going to—"

She ran her tongue over the tip again. "Isn't that the point?"

"Oh gosh." He eased his grip on her hair and Syn continued her exploration, bringing him to the brink again. This time, when his strong fingers knotted and tugged on her tresses, they guided the pace. And when he came, he murmured the word "Mine."

The music from the concert blared and Tristan tried to figure out how in the world he could have been so stupid. Two days with her and he was attached. He had one day left with Syn and he sure as hell didn't want to give her up. After what she'd just done to him in the limo, there was no way he'd ever be able to look at her and not think about her mouth on him. About the way she used her tongue to tease. About how open she'd been with him all weekend. That was the Syn he would see forever. That was the Syn he wanted to see. The one who was happy and smiling and teasing. This version of her made him laugh. Okay, sure, she still drove him insane, but in a completely different way. To go back to what they used to be wouldn't work. He didn't want to let her go. And that irritated him. This was supposed to be fun and no strings, and now he was adding strings? *Come on, keep it together.*

They had a private viewing box for the show. It was designed for a small group of six or so, but as it was, with just them, it seemed like a private concert. In the other viewing boxes, couples and friends and groups all danced and partied.

Syn laughed as she danced and Tristan wanted to remember her like this. With her head tossed back and a grin on her face and freedom in her eyes.

She moved against him and he fell into the beat behind her. Wrapping his arms around her, he held on tight. As she danced, the dress slipped up and she tugged it back down. Every time another bare inch of thigh was revealed, he prayed for more, and then she'd just calmly pull it back down again.

Their waitress brought them a bottle of champagne. He tipped her well and asked for privacy. If he only had another twenty-four hours or so with Syn, he wanted privacy, and a lot of it. The way the viewing boxes were set up, there were ten on each side of the stage. Five stacked on top of another five. And each box had a small sitting area and a balcony. The stone railings came up to chest height on all sides.

While the DJ thumped a heavy hip-hop-infused pop beat, they danced and Tristan slid his fingertips just under Syn's skirt. She paid him no attention, just continued moving to the beat.

He brushed her thick hair off the nape of her neck and kissed her softly. "I want to touch you."

"I want to be touched. I wore this dress for a reason."

In that moment, he realized that she played the game better than he did. She'd been weaving a web of seduction around him all night, slowly driving him mad. Now he was so desperate for her he might burst.

Tristan slid his fingers up her satiny inner thigh until he reached the apex of her thighs and the silken heat between.

When he slid a finger inside her, she grabbed the ledge. Down below, Coco belted out her latest hit and thousands of people danced and sang along. All the while, he slowly penetrated Syn, teasing her slick opening. Tormented himself.

She reached behind her and tugged on his belt. Knowing what she wanted, what she needed, what they both craved, he yanked his wallet out and grabbed a condom. With several swift movements, she had his erection out of his pants and he sheathed himself in seconds.

Syn held on to the railing and shifted her stance to make room for him between her thighs.

Tristan grazed his teeth against the nape of her neck. "What are you doing to me?"

"I don't know," she whispered.

And while Coco sang "I'm Yours" he drove into Syn. The sharp bite of ecstasy was quick to take hold. Would it always be like this with her? Would he keep wanting her this bad as if he'd never had her? With each slide home and retreat, he marked her as his. With the crescendo of the music and the thump of the bass, he took her and she took him until he didn't know where she ended and he began.

Chapter 11

Synthia woke up with Tristan's hand over her heart. For several long moments she just let herself enjoy being in his arms. As if maybe in an alternative universe she could just wake up like this and everything would be okay. And she could be happy and not have to do everything alone.

Tristan kissed her shoulder. "I don't want to wake up. Let's stay here and pretend we don't have to go back." Playing with a lock of her hair, he added, "I'm going to miss the Vegas cocoon."

Thread by thread the fantasy began to unravel. Icy dread mixed with frosty admonishment crawled up her spine. *Vegas cocoon. You knew better than to get attached to him.* She'd known this was temporary, but over the past couple of days she'd thought—well, never mind what she thought. "I need to start getting ready," she murmured. This was Tristan and this was a fling. Outside of this, they didn't work. They were too different. This only worked now because it was in a suspended reality.

She shifted, but he only held her tighter. "No," he whispered. "Not yet." The unspoken words between them hung in the air.

Her heart squeezed. She'd let herself get too close. "Tristan…" She let her voice trail.

He nuzzled her neck. "Yeah, Syn?"

"You sure do hold on tight, don't you?"

He kissed her neck and he loosened his grip a little. "Didn't mean to crush you."

Syn smirked. "If this was the old Tristan, I'm not sure I would believe you."

"Mostly I just wanted to touch you." His voice was soft, almost inaudible.

Deep emotion curled around her heart. He'd never told her that before. She wanted to believe him because, she realized, she never wanted to leave. She wanted to be in his arms. Wanted to believe that they could work. *Don't believe the hype, Syn*. In bed, they were fantastic. But outside bed, it wouldn't be possible. They were too different, and believing in that fairy tale could cost her this project.

Never mind the warmth she felt in her heart when she was with him. She wasn't going to let him hurt her. She couldn't. It was time to take this experience and lock it into a deep box far away. She wasn't going to let this affect her. *Vegas cocoon*. She wasn't going to let him hurt her.

Syn rolled over and kissed him softly on the lips. "I think it's time to return to the real world now."

His gaze searched hers. He frowned but whispered softly, "Okay."

This was a mistake. *Had* been a mistake. He'd been a fool to think this thing with him and Syn would be some casual get-each-other-out-of-their-systems fling. Now it was Monday morning and she'd slid out of bed an hour ago.

And just like that, they were back to normal. As if this had never happened. As if he'd never gotten to see this side of her. She was once again the enemy. Well, he hoped not. Even if this situation was merely temporary, he didn't want to be on the attack with her. They had to find a way to coexist, didn't they?

After a cold shower designed to wake his brain up and to cool his libido, he'd dressed quickly and gone looking for Syn. Her usual pencil skirt and blouse combo were back. Paired with some do-me pumps that he hadn't seen before. Gone was the loose, flowing hair he'd seen since Friday. The characteristic bun was back in place. And the sweet, sexy makeup was gone. Instead she'd gone back to her usual red lips and a cool attitude. "Any chance there's coffee?" *Oh, great, that was the best you could offer.*

She whirled to meet his gaze. Her expression was all soft parted lips and surprised wide eyes, as if she hadn't expected him to be awake so early. He hadn't had much choice. Once she was out of bed, he hadn't been able to sleep.

"Good morning. Yeah, um, there's some coffee. Room service brought it up a few minutes ago."

Her tone was cordial but distant. His Syn was gone. "Thanks," he muttered.

She shifted in those killer heels of hers. "I wasn't sure if we were heading over to the airport together or not. If you'd rather go separately, I can—"

He ground his teeth together and shook his head. "No, together is fine. I'll grab a to-go cup and we can head out now."

"No rush. The valet already came to collect our bags."

Hell. This was almost worse than the dreaded egg-shells he'd been hoping to avoid and the battling war gods they'd once been. "For heaven's sake, Syn, can we talk about this?"

She rolled her shoulders. "Sorry. I know this is awkward. I clearly didn't think this out. I have no idea how to act around you now."

Tristan sighed. "Okay, how about we act normally?"

"Well, have you forgotten that normal for us includes shouting and eye sex?"

His dick twitched. *Down, boy.* "Okay, normal but without the shouting. I don't want this to be weird and awkward. Maybe we could even try being friends."

She relaxed her shoulders. "Friends…you say that like it's easy. We couldn't manage friends before and now you think that we've seen each other naked, it'll be any easier?"

She did have a point there. "Not exactly, but this over-polite shit is going to kill me. Not to mention it's a dead giveaway."

Her eyebrows snapped down. "Pardon me for not knowing the etiquette. This was your idea, remember?"

Tristan sighed. "Yeah, I know, I just—"

There was a knock at the door. Synthia inhaled. "Looks like our car is here."

Synthia's stride was as brisk and direct as always and the pencil skirt hugged her ass just right, giving him a spectacular view. He didn't want it to end like this. Once in the elevator, he turned to her. "Syn, are you okay?"

Her gaze was flat, without any of the fire of before Vegas and missing the heat of the past few days. "Fine. This was the agreement, right? We go back to normal, whatever that is, now. Don't worry, I'll figure it out."

She didn't meet his gaze. "Look at me."

She didn't comply. Instead she kept her eyes glued to the lit floor numbers. The elevator slowed and dinged and the doors opened. Immediately Tristan assumed proper elevator positioning, sliding around next to her and looking straight ahead. Like her, he also held on to the back rail for support. As people filed in they were pressed closer and closer together, their fingertips nearly touching. That span of an inch separating his index finger from hers might as well have been the Grand Canyon. The tension twirled around them, thickening and swirling. On the first-floor pool deck everyone filed out, leaving the two of them alone. Tristan stared down at their fingertips. She met his gaze. Her almond-shaped dark eyes blinking up at him. The decision was already made for him. If this was the way they were going to be with each other, he wanted one more taste before he had to let her go.

When he wound his arms around her waist, her eyes rounded in shock. "Tristan—"

He didn't let her finish the thought; instead he kissed her. The spark that flared between them flickered and his blood rushed. Her response was instant. She groaned and slid her hands into his hair. Her tongue glided against his and he shuddered.

Tristan pulled the pin out of her hair, moaning as her heavy tresses fell over his fingertips. Synthia melded her body to his, arching into his caress.

When the elevator dinged again, she staggered back. He reached for her, but she stepped just out of range. Her chin tilted up and just like that, the mask was back. When she stalked out at the next floor, he didn't stop her.

Chapter 12

Ten days, twelve hours and twenty-two minutes since she'd returned from Vegas and Synthia *still* hadn't recovered from the storm that was Tristan Dawson. She couldn't turn around in the office without seeing him, and forget about sleeping because every time she closed her eyes, there he was, taunting her.

The dreams she could deal with. At least they weren't public knowledge. But the days at work had become a version of water torture.

The two of them had retreated to their separate corners as usual, but they didn't even speak. And if they did, it was with that tight politeness she'd instituted in Vegas.

She finally understood. All those women she'd seen falling at his feet and practically, if not literally, throwing themselves at him, she got it. She was a member of that fan club. Even had the damn T-shirt.

But now that was all over and she was supposed to

just pretend it never happened? She wasn't *that* good. It didn't help that sometimes she'd catch him looking at her. And not in the hot, speculative way he used to, but more in the hot "I know what you taste like and I want some more" kind of way.

A brief knock on her door brought her out of her reverie and Olivia sauntered in without knocking. "Do you want to tell me what in the world is going on with you and Tristan Dawson?"

Oh, crap. Lying was not one of her skills. But she didn't want to go into it. Liv would give her the "Are you out of your damn mind?" look, then possibly slap her for her stupidity.

"What do you mean?"

Olivia frowned as she scrutinized her. "Well, for starters, you guys haven't had a single knock-down, drag-out fight in nearly two weeks. I keep popcorn in my desk just for those occasions. Second, you two were entirely too polite to each other in this morning's staff meeting. Third, I just got the word from Bryan that the new Wilkinson campaign is a go and I asked Tristan if he would try to wrestle you for the client and all he did was shake his head and say you deserved it. Not to mention the way he's been staring at you. Girl, it's hotter than ever. If he looked at me that way, I might forget he's a walking advertisement for Trojan and jump his bones." Liv sank into the leather seat across from her. "So spill."

When in doubt deny. "Sorry, Liv, I don't know what you're talking about."

"Bull." She leaned forward, pointing an accusatory finger her way. "And you're a bad liar, so don't even start. What in the world happened in Vegas?"

Syn sighed. "Would you believe we buried something in the desert?"

"I'd only believe that if it was his dead body. C'mon, what's with you?"

"We sort of called a truce, buried the hatchet."

Olivia's eyebrows shot up. "And by bury, do you mean bone?"

"Liv!"

"Honey, I'm just saying the intense gazes, the way you guys *don't* look at each other… This reeks of—" Liv's mouth dropped open. "Oh my, you really *did* sleep with him."

"Would you keep your voice down?" Synthia whispered. "I do not need this getting out."

Liv leaned forward and muttered in an exaggerated whisper, "I'll keep my voice down if you tell me the truth. Consider me a vault of information."

Heat spread over Synthia's skin as she said, "Fine. I slept with him."

Olivia blinked. Her mouth moved, but nothing came out. Finally she shook her head and tried again. "Okay, first things first… How was it?"

Syn nodded. "He's every bit as good as he thinks he is."

Liv fake-swooned. "Oh God. Is it okay that I'm equal parts mortified and equal parts totally jealous?"

"Yeah, I'm mortified too. Well, more mortified that I was so reckless. Now we're having to deal with the aftermath."

"Okay, start from the beginning. Leave nothing out."

As Synthia recounted the story, Olivia sat forward listening intently. Finally she spoke. "So you want to sleep with him again."

Yes. "No. Of course not. It's better this way. It's just awkward. I mean, I don't have flings. I keep it professional. This is my career, my life."

"I mean, you said you sort of like him."

"I said I understand him better. He's not so bad." *And* she liked him.

"So you're saying there's no way you're going to enjoy him now that you're back?"

Syn sighed. "Well, he made it pretty clear that it was only temporary, and I don't know what I want. And this is my career we're talking about. I don't need the gossip. I want to be judged on my work and not who I was dumb enough to sleep with." Even if she did want him so bad the weaker part of her wasn't opposed to begging.

"Everyone knows how good you are, Syn."

"Trust me, they'll forget. Soon enough, *this* will be the narrative. Besides, he was temporary. More important, I was just another girl in the long line of temporary for him."

Olivia frowned. "Maybe you weren't. He looks like he's pretty beat up about something."

Syn tilted her chin up. "I promise you it isn't me."

Tristan tried to keep his focus. It was hard enough that he had a lot to prepare for the Bliss presentation, but every time he thought his head was clear, Syn would work her way in. They'd managed to keep their distance, but it wasn't exactly easy. Staff meetings were mandatory, but he'd taken to slipping in just before they started so he could avoid her. Unfortunately today it seemed that she had the same idea. Cue awkward dance in the doorway, where her perfume had swirled around him making him foggy and incoherent for several seconds. He'd been completely useless the rest of the day.

Now with everyone gone for the day, he could finally get some work done.

Stacking his material, he headed to the conference

room for more space. He wanted to spread out to look at what he'd pulled for his presentation. Every office and cube on this half of the floor was dark.

He turned the corner to find the lights in the conference room already on. What the? "Hey, is anyone still here—"

He halted short and took in the view, a woman bent over the table and fiddled with the projector, her leather pencil skirt pulled tight over her taut behind. *Syn.* She jumped with surprise and whirled around. "Tristan. I didn't know anyone else was still here."

He tried to swallow around the sawdust in his mouth. In Vegas he'd been fool enough to think he could forget about everything that had happened. He knew better now. He wanted her, but more than that, he wanted to *be* with her.

"Sorry. Didn't mean to surprise you." He set down his binders and charts on the long rectangular table. "Do you need help with the projector?" If she was working in here, he'd have to use the smaller conference room at the end of the hall.

"I think I got it." She turned round again and stretched to reach the last cable. With each stretch, the fabric pulled over her butt again and he groaned.

She froze. For a long breath neither of them moved. She met his gaze in the reflection of the window. Her lips parted and her tongue peeked out to moisten her lips. When she sucked her bottom lip in and grazed it with her teeth, his tenuous hold on his control snapped.

He slid his hand up over her back, and then back down over her ass. Her breath came out as a little huff and she widened her stance.

His voice was thick as he spoke. "I can't get you out of my head."

"What happened to going back to normal?"

With shaking hands, he bracketed her hips and slowly turned her around to face him. "I was clearly an idiot."

He paused just a breath from kissing her. A shudder ran through her body and she parted her lips. "What are you doing?"

"Something I've been thinking about doing since we got back."

The kiss started off sweet. Just a peck, their lips barely even touching. More of an exchange of breaths. But then he kissed her again, and the same dangerous spark that had ignited between them in Vegas grew and spread, until his skin itched with the need to touch her.

Tentatively she touched her tongue to his and it took all his control not to take over the kiss. She was testing him out. Seeing if she could trust him. With a soft moan she settled into the kiss, dipping her tongue into his mouth, toying with his. She wound her hands into his hair, drawing him to her, closer, arching her body into his.

He released her for the briefest of moments to lock the door and ensure their privacy. Then with trembling hands, he released the pin that held her bun together. For two weeks he'd been dying to do that. To see his Syn, the secret Syn, the one no one else knew. One hand toyed with the silken tresses while the other fumbled with the buttons on her blouse. The deep V had taunted him all through the staff meeting.

She helped out by tugging her blouse out of her skirt, and then she went for the zipper on his jeans.

The only sound that permeated the silence of the conference room was his moans as she scored her nails down his back. Followed by her mewling sounds when he yanked down the cups of her delicate bra, freeing her breasts.

Tristan tore his lips from her. "Wow, I missed you."

He kissed his way along her jawline to the column of her neck, to her collarbone and finally to her breast. Full and ripe, the chocolate-tipped peaks beckoned to him. Gently he laid her back on the conference table and stepped deeper between her legs. Dipping his head, he hovered just over one nipple, gently blowing on it. She arched her back into him impatiently. He pulled a dark bud into his mouth and she called out, "Tristan."

He suckled gently and she rolled her hips against him impatiently.

Sliding his hands under her skirt, he paused for a moment just as his fingers approached her soft center. "Are there any surprises here for me?"

Harsh breaths tore from her throat. "Maybe."

"I do like surprises."

He slid a finger past her panty line and growled. "I see you're still smooth."

"Surprise."

Chuckling, Tristan hooked his finger in her panties and tugged down. She scooted to the edge, lifting her hips to help him. He released her breast and pulled back. Lowering himself to his knees, he hiked her skirt all the way up.

The heather-soft skin of her sex glistened with moisture. Beckoning him. When he licked her, her hips bucked off the table and he wrapped his hands around her thighs to keep them wide.

He took his time stroking her soft folds with his tongue while he teased her clit with his thumb.

As he tasted and teased, he knew the moment she was close. The quiver in her legs always gave it away. Pulling back and standing, his movements hurried yet efficient, he retrieved a condom and sheathed himself.

Syn watched him intently, and he didn't tear his gaze from hers.

Tristan joined their bodies. Inch by inch, he slid into her silken depths, losing a piece of himself as he went.

One word buzzed through his head as her body stroked his cock like a pulsing glove. *Home.*

Chapter 13

Synthia tried not to watch Tristan as they sat in on the client meeting. But her body betrayed her, and every thirty seconds or so she'd accidentally meet his gaze and he would wink at her.

Her phone buzzed in her palm and she glanced down at it.

Tristan: Meet me at Griffith Park Observatory tonight.

Synthia: Why?

Tristan: I want to talk to you.

Synthia: You're not giving me I-want-to-talk-to-you-eyes right now.

She glanced up at him and even though his eyes were trained on Bryan, he grinned. Her phone buzzed again.

Tristan: What eyes am I giving you?

Heat flushed her body. She'd ignore him. How hard could it be really? That way he wouldn't wink at her and graze his bottom lip with his teeth or make her remember last night. And of course her mind, like her body, was in no mood to behave as a memory of the previous night flashed. After they'd made love, he stayed inside her. She'd felt every pulse, every twitch. He'd held her and kissed her softly, whispering, "I miss you," in her ear.

Bryan turned to her. "Synthia, will you and Tristan be ready to present this Friday? Bella will be coming into the office. She's been in Italy for the last two weeks, so this is the best she can do."

Syn nodded. "I can be ready."

Tristan nodded, as well. "I'll be ready too." Bryan turned his attention to the remainder of the employees and continued discussing quarterly numbers and new client business.

Syn's phone buzzed again.

Tristan: I was serious when I said we had to talk last night.

Synthia: Not a good idea.

Tristan: Please, I'll behave.

She smiled and narrowed her eyes at him. His expression of mock innocence didn't fool her. But she was curious and they *did* need to talk. He made her reckless and she didn't want a repeat of last night. *Yes, you do.* Okay, fair enough, but she didn't want it under those circumstances again. And the more she ignored him, the more out of control she'd feel. She texted back, Fine, but I'll meet you there. A shadow crossed over his expression quickly, but it was gone so fast she might have imagined it.

Tristan: Fine. Just as long as you meet me.

That night, she dressed carefully, since she wasn't sure of how things would end up with them. Skinny jeans, a silk blouse, and a blazer with boots. The only concession to semidate status she made was to wear her hair down.

He waited for her outside, pacing in front of the entrance. "Am I late?"

Relief chased a grin as he saw her. "No. I guess I was a little early."

She rolled her shoulders, willing them to relax. "So... what did you want to talk about?"

He leaned into her. "Are we really going to pretend last night didn't happen?"

She sighed. "I'm not sure what you want from me, Tristan. It feels like you're playing a game with me and I have to tell you, I don't know the rules."

He took her hand. "I'm not playing a game with you. I swear." He rubbed the back of his neck. "I haven't got a clue how to do this, but here it is. I want to be with you."

She frowned and tried to tug her hand back. "You mean you want an affair."

Tristan stroked his thumb over the back of her hand. "No. I mean I want to be with you. Yes, I can't seem to keep my hands off you, but I also want the parts of you where you laugh and you stick your hair in a giant ponytail on top of your head before you sleep, and the part where you fight with me and call me a moron, and the part where you dance when you think no one is watching, and the part of you that lights up when you do something a little dangerous or naughty. I want to *be* with you. I was kidding myself in Vegas. There's no compartmentalizing my feelings for you and I was crazy to try."

Her heart hammered and the blood rushed in her ears. "I don't know what to say."

He chuckled and let his head hang. "Okay, let me walk you through it. This is the part where you tell me how you feel. Maybe this was just a Vegas thing for you. Maybe last night was a mistake and you want nothing to do with me."

"Tristan, I didn't say that."

He released her hand. "Then tell me what you're thinking. I can't read you. In Vegas it was so easy, but now I can't make out all the nuances. You have to tell me something. Anything. Tell me it was all a mistake. Tell me you don't want to see me anymore. Or better yet, tell me you can't sleep without me next to you either. Tell me you think about me during the day and you spend half your days hoping you'll run into me. But you have to tell me. I can't guess."

"Tristan, I—" She dragged in a breath. "I'm scared."

He shook his head. "What are you so afraid of, Syn?"

"That you'll break my heart." The moment the words were out, she wished she could call them back.

He stepped in front of her and stroked a thumb over her cheek. "I'm not going to hurt you. I wouldn't do that."

Tears pricked her eyes and she blinked them away rapidly. "I just—I don't know how to do *this*."

"I know." He drew her into his body, and cradled her cheek in his palm. "All I'm looking for is for you to take a chance on me."

His voice, his scent, the strength of his body. All those elements combined to weave a spell around her.

She wanted him. If she was honest with herself, she'd admit that she always had. But could she do this? Jump in with him? *Yeah. Oh yeah.*

The alternative, not being with him, sucked. She'd tried that for two weeks and she wasn't a huge fan. But trust didn't come easy and he was still Tristan Dawson. "If we do this, how do we do this?" She pointed a finger back and forth between them. "At work? You'll be insulated from gossip and stuff, but I won't. Last night was—" She flushed. "Well, you were there, it was pretty awesome, but I'm not that woman. We can't—"

"I completely agree. It was too risky. We'll use discretion, and while sneaking around is hot, I'd rather not hide."

She expelled a breath. "I need to take things slow. I'm not sure I can just jump into a relationship."

Tristan ran his hands through his hair. "We'll take it slow. Glacial even. Whatever you want. I just want a chance with you. I'll take what I can get."

"Tristan, are you sure you want to do this? With my trust issues and your panty-dropping smile, this isn't exactly going to be easy. It's a big step."

He grinned. "Panty-dropping, huh?" He laughed but sobered quickly. "How about this? We'll take it one step at a time. Nice and easy. We can start by me taking you on a date. Simple. And we'll work on the trust thing."

For the second time in less than a month, Synthia ignored the warning bells of caution. She wanted to be with him. Tugging on his lapels, she kissed him.

Chapter 14

A night out with her sister was long overdue. Being with Tristan made her realize that she'd spent a lot of time being a mom and she needed to throttle back and have some fun.

"Honestly you look happy, Syn."

Syn took a sip of her martini and smiled at her sister. "I feel happy. It had been a while since everything was going this great."

"And you're not worried at all about this week?"

"Nope. Tristan and I went over the presentations. They complement each other. Instead of trying to one-up each other, for once. I think it'll go well."

Xia grinned. "I like him. Or rather I like you with him."

"Was that before or after he gave you all the men advice?" Tristan had come over the other night for dinner and met Xia, who had peppered him with questions about dating.

"Okay, well, both. I mean, he's pretty to look at. And I mean smoking hot. But he's thoughtful and nice. I hope I didn't ruin your groove thing the other night when I told him stories about us growing up."

Syn barked out a laugh. "Even *I'm* not saying groove thing anymore."

Xia put up one finger. "I'm bringing it back. And it was nice being the big sister to you for once and checking out your new man. I was ready to give him the hairy eyeball at a moment's notice."

Syn took another sip of her drink. "Look at you, all grown up."

Xia preened. "I know, right. Can you believe it?" She leaned forward. "So, what's the word on tall, dark and ridiculously rich?"

"Xia!"

"What, it's true, right? I mean, he *is* a Dawson."

"He's not like the other Dawsons. For starters, he doesn't work for the family business."

Xia raised her eyebrow. "A hard worker, huh? Looks like he knows the way to my sister's heart."

"Yeah, okay," Syn laughed. "I'm a sucker for someone driven. And it turns out I was wrong about him."

Xai's lips formed a perfect O as she lifted her eyebrows in a mock shocked face. "You don't say."

"I can admit when I'm wrong."

"Not the, quote, 'womanizing idiotic playboy' you thought he was?"

Okay, so maybe she'd been a little harsh, but in her defense that was before she'd actually known him properly. But when he was with her, she certainly had all his attention.

"It sounds like love to me."

Syn coughed on her drink, and alcohol burned her nasal cavity. "Who said anything about love?"

"Oh my God, are you still on your antilove kick? You better not screw this up, Syn. I haven't seen you this happy in like ever and you're certainly more chilled out than you usually are."

"I'm not screwing it up." But fear slipped in past her defenses before she could shore up the line. "We're taking it slow. Not jumping into anything too quickly, getting to know each other."

"I don't know what for. I mean, you're spending every spare minute you can with him and I went to your place two nights in a row last week and you weren't there. I only assume you stayed at his."

A flush crept up Syn's neck as she remembered just what they'd been getting up to at his place. He really did have a very talented tongue. But just how did he come by it? She slammed the thought to the back corner of the dark part of her mind. She was going to ignore it and have fun. She liked fun. She could do fun. Right?

Xia didn't seem to notice her distress. "Just as long as you're following the same rules he gave me the other night. Granted, by the way he treats you, you have a good one. I'm happy for you."

Syn couldn't help going through all the advice Tristan had given Xia. He'd told her to find a guy who put her first and treated her with respect.

He hadn't told a soul at work about them. They'd even gone back to normal at work. Well, if normal meant he was nice to her and professional without the awkwardness. Of course, the moment they were alone, he was all kinds of inappropriate.

"I'm happy for me too. And we'll see where it goes." *Liar, you love him.* A tight band squeezed around her chest. That scared the hell out of her. She'd started to fall for him before Vegas. That was their dance. She'd always appreciated some aspects of his personality, but she'd never considered the whole person before Vegas.

Oh God, she was in love, with Tristan Dawson...

Xia watched her carefully. "You look like you swallowed a bug. Did you just realize you love him?"

Synthia swallowed hard. "Is it that obvious?"

Xia nodded. "I knew it the second you were sulking around when you got back from Vegas. It looked like a breakup mope. No woman acts like that unless she loves a guy."

"Well, now what?"

Xia laughed. "Well, now you tell him."

Syn frowned. "What if he doesn't love me back?"

Xia reached over and squeezed her hand. "Don't be ridiculous. He's the lucky one. And he knows it."

Syn had never been in love before. Was this how it felt? She wasn't entirely sure she liked the feeling.

Xia jumped up. "I'm going to get us another drink."

Syn shook her head. "No. You sit. I'm buying. My way of saying we should do this more often." And clearing her head.

"I'm not turning down free drinks."

"Of course you aren't. Your sister didn't raise no fool."

"Tris, where the hell you been, man? I haven't seen your sorry ass since before you left for Vegas. It's been nearly a month. I was worried that you'd gotten married without a prenup and some grifter had you chained up in a basement in her house."

Tristan laughed and nudged his brother's shoulder. "Sorry I missed the big dinner, man. I've just been busy with work."

Taylor eyed him. "I'm calling you out. Work doesn't keep you *that* busy."

He shrugged. "Well, maybe I have something worthwhile to work toward."

Taylor clamped a hand over his heart. "Say it ain't so." Then he frowned. "Actually I did mention to the old man about how hard you've been working and your new project."

Tristan scowled at his brother. "Why would you do that?"

"Sorry. You know how he can be. I thought it was all curiosity, and then he started grilling me about your big presentation."

This was the last thing Tristan needed. "Taylor, you know how manipulative he is."

His shoulders drew up. "Look, I'm sorry. I'll make it up to you. I just thought, finally, he gave a damn for something other than his own purposes. It's possible."

"Don't count on it." Tristan cracked his neck, then drew in a deep breath. "Don't worry about it. I'm not mad at you. Just touchy. Before I left for Vegas, he called with the same old song and dance. It made me a little edgy where he's concerned. As if I can't see his ploy for what it is. I come fully into my trust fund next year when I turn twenty-seven. Which means I also inherit Grandpa's voting shares. He just wants me where he can control me."

"Cynical much?" Then he added, "How was Vegas anyway? Usually you're back from a trip like that regaling me with tales of debauchery. This time, nothing."

Tristan sipped his scotch. "You know it was a work trip, right?"

"And you know you're a Dawson, right? You don't have to work if you don't want to. Life is meant to be enjoyed, *especially* if you're in Vegas."

Tristan shook his head. How could they be so different but so close? "Actually I'm seeing someone. I've known her for a while."

Taylor's eyebrows rose. "What? Who? Is it that blonde girl from the club?"

"What? No way!"

Taylor smiled. "That was quick. So, what's she like, your girl? And when do I get to meet her and show her some of the Dawson charm?"

Note to self, Taylor was never meeting Syn. Not because he didn't trust his brother. More like that he didn't trust his brother not to embarrass him. "Uh, not for a while if you keep talking like that."

Taylor nodded, suddenly solemn. "So you actually like her, then?"

"I do. She's smart. A hell of a lot smarter than me. But don't tell her I said that. Because she'll never let me live it down."

"I like the sounds of her already."

"And she's funny. Snarky sense of humor. Careful not to piss her off because the verbal smackdown will scar you. But she can also be very sweet. She's tough, you know."

Taylor gave him a knowing smile. "Sounds like love, little brother."

Love? Something squeezed around his heart. The feeling wasn't altogether unpleasant. But it felt a little like fear, but not the blinding terror that immobilized you, more like the fear of losing something.

"I don't know. But she's pretty special."

"And where did you meet this paragon of virtue and beauty, and does she have a sister?"

Oh no, Tristan was *not* doing that to Xia. Though Xia would take his brother well in hand. Especially now that she was armed with his guy-dating tactics and maneuvers. "She does have a sister, but she's too young for you. And I met Syn at work."

Taylor's eyebrows snapped down. "Sin? Are you sure you don't work at a strip club?"

Tristan rolled his eyes. "Synthia, *S-Y-N*."

"Wait, is this that woman who was giving you such a hard time? The mouthy one?"

Tristan laughed. "Yeah, that's her."

"And you somehow managed to convince her to go out with you? I thought that girl hated you?"

"She just didn't know how awesome I was yet."

"And how pray tell did you make her see the light?"

"Vegas changed everything."

Taylor gave him a knowing smile. "I'll bet it did. You know—"

"Tristan, is that you?"

Tristan whirled around, hearing the familiar voice. "Bella?" He barely recognized the Bliss Hotel magnate. She wore a short black dress that displayed all her assets. As if she was begging the world to notice her. But she missed the mark. Too short, too tight and too revealing. It all amounted to trying too hard.

"Bella? What are you doing here?"

Her grin was wide. "I was meeting a friend for dinner, but he's otherwise engaged for a moment." She swayed into him and he picked up on the alcohol on her breath.

Taylor wasted no time at all. "Don't mind my brother, he's very rude. Would you like to join us for a drink?"

She smiled up at both of them with her unfocused eyes. "Sure." She smiled cheekily at Taylor. "What are you buying me to drink, handsome?"

"What would you like to drink? And it's Taylor."

"Ketel One, neat. Taylor and Tristan." She eyed them

both up and down. "They sure do make you Dawson boys easy on the eyes."

She slurred her words, and Tristan made a mental note to cut off her drinks after this one. He didn't know how much she'd had to drink, but slurring meant it had probably already been one drink too many.

When her drink arrived, Taylor handed it to her with a smile. "So, where has my brother been keeping you?"

She patted a hand on Taylor's chest before taking a sip. She pouted a little. "Tristan, I'm disappointed you didn't tell your brother about me. Seeing as we could be working together soon."

He cleared his throat and shifted uncomfortably. "Bella is a client, Tay."

Taylor straightened immediately. "Oh, what kind of client?"

Bella's smile was lazy. "My family owns Bliss Hotels. I'm the vice president of Marketing and Operations." She turned to Tristan, reaching up to cup his face. "And your brother here hasn't taken the bait and asked me out yet."

Oh, shit. How the hell did he wiggle out of this gracefully and leave her pride intact? "As beautiful as you are, Bella, I don't date clients."

She leaned in to whisper in his ear, "That's really too bad. I was looking forward to seeing what else you could do for me besides market analysis."

"Bella—"

Bella pursed her lips and held up a hand to stop him. "So I take it this *isn't* going to happen?"

He shook his head. "No. I'm sorry."

"You have a thing for Synthia Michaels."

How the hell had she known that? "Yeah. We sort of have a thing."

"I had a feeling. That first day at Stellar Reach, I could

see the tension between you. I wondered if sending you to Vegas together was a good idea. I figured you'd either learn to get along or destroy each other. I guess you learned to get along."

Tristan ground his teeth. He didn't want this impacting Syn's chances of getting the job. "Syn is really good at what she does. In a lot of ways better than me. You should really consider her fairly for the job."

Bella's eyes narrowed. "As pretty as you are, let me promise you that I will always look at the bottom line and do the best for my company."

Tristan nodded. "As long as we understand each other. I just want it to be a fair playing field for the both of us."

Bella nodded. "It'll be fair." She shrugged. "I can't say I'm not disappointed, though." One of the other bar patrons jostled Bella and she lost her balance, throwing herself onto Tristan for support. He steadied her quickly, but she still wobbled. "You okay?"

"Yeah." She lifted her head. "I guess I'm not the only one who's unsteady on their feet."

Prickly heat made the hairs on the back of his neck stand up. The sudden sense of awareness had him looking around for who might be watching him.

The moment his gaze met Syn's from across the crowded lounge, he froze. Her gaze dipped from his eyes to Bella pressed up against him, then back to his eyes.

Then her beautiful, lively dark eyes went flat and cold, just before she turned and stalked away.

"Damn."

Chapter 15

Synthia didn't even stop to think. All she knew was the cloying darkness and pain that wrapped around her heart. So much for him caring about her. He was still the same old Tristan.

She ran right past her sister, whose attention had been taken by a guy in a suit, and into the fresh air of the night. Outside the lounge, the traffic sounds were nearly as loud as the music inside, but at least she could breathe easier.

She braced herself when she heard the slapping shoes on concrete. He was following her. Fight or flight, fight or flight. Syn turned on her heels and met his gaze.

Tristan stopped short. "Syn, let me explain. It's not what you think."

She forced a calm into her voice she didn't feel. She *would not* be the crazy, out-of-control woman. She *would* use her grown-up words. She *would not* kick him in the nuts. Well, she couldn't be certain about that last part. "I can't do this right now," she muttered.

"Syn, just talk to me. Don't crawl up into your shell and shut me out. I know you saw me with Bella, but you have to know I wouldn't do that."

"I know what I saw. But you know what, even if it wasn't what I thought, this still boils down to me. I can't be in a relationship with someone like you. I'll always be waiting for the other shoe to drop. I never should have said yes.

He dug his hands into his hair as he paced. "This is crazy. You're using a total misunderstanding as a reason to run." He glared at her, then squared his shoulders. When he shoved his hands in his pockets his jaw twitched.

Tears picked her eyes and she blinked them back. "I have to protect myself. You have the power to hurt me and I can't let you. This has gotten way out of control."

"Syn, come on. I've shown you the real me. You're the only person who actually knows me. Don't give up."

"I don't have a choice, Tristan. If I keep doing this with you, I'm going to get burned."

"Jealously and fear are clouding your brain. You're smarter than this."

"I have to go."

Before she could turn away, he reached for her. He planted both hands on her face, his caress warm and gentle. Tristan sucked in a deep breath, then stepped forward into her space. She automatically took a step back and glared at him.

"Synthia, I'm in love with you."

Her breath caught in her throat as she blinked up at him.

"I know every single smile you have. I would never use you. I'm not that guy. And I don't know how else to prove that to you. And honestly I don't think I *can* ever prove that to you. You need to be open to this, to us. I love you. I've been dancing around finding a way to your heart for two years. And you feel something for me too. Or else you wouldn't be running scared. But until you trust me, this can't work."

Tears stung her eyes and she blinked them away rapidly as she wrapped her arms around herself. "I'm sorry. I can't."

He sniffed and rubbed his nose with a knuckle. "You know where to find me if you want to start believing in somebody."

Chapter 16

Tristan turned off the water in the shower in time to hear his phone ringing in his bedroom. Maybe it was Syn. After their argument, he'd called a few times to talk to her, but no luck. How had things gotten so screwed up? *Because you should have told her how you felt sooner.*

Well, he *had* told her. If he'd told her how he felt at the beginning, would she even have gone to Vegas with him? Would that night in the elevator have happened? Maybe she would have given him a shot. *Maybe not.*

But instead of Syn, it was his father.

"Dad?" He frowned.

"I hope this isn't a bad time." His voice was gruff.

If his father was calling him at home, something was going on. "What's the matter, Dad?"

"It's your mother. She had an accident."

The breath rushed out of his lungs. "I'm on my way."

"Tristan, we're in Santa Barbara."

"What?" His parents lived in Beverly Hills. They did have a vacation house up north, though.

"It happened at the house."

"Fine, text me the hospital info." He hung up without another word and tossed on the nearest clothing he could find and didn't give a thought to how wrinkled it might be. The two-hour drive north was made in a haze.

When he finally got to the hospital, his father met him in the waiting room.

"Dad, what happened?"

He frowned. "Your mother fell down the stairs at the new house."

His stomach dropped. "Oh no."

Tristan's father held up a hand. "Don't overreact. She'll be fine."

Tristan curled his hands into fists. Then forced himself to unfurl them. This was deliberate. The old man had used his mother to get him out of LA and away from that presentation. Fury bubbled under his skin. He'd deal with his father later. "Where is she?"

The old man sighed. "Room 102."

When he arrived at his mother's room, she turned to him with a smile. "Oh, Tristan, I told your father not to call you. I know you had that big presentation going on today."

"It's okay. My co-presenter will handle it. Do you want to tell me what happened?"

"It was silly. I fell off a ladder as I was trying to install a new chandelier and lost my balance. He shouldn't have called. He knew how important today was for you. Taylor told him. You could have come after."

His stomach sank. It didn't matter now anyway. He was here and his mom looked okay, but she was in traction, so it was serious. And he was glad he'd come. "Don't worry about it. I should be here and I am." He just prayed Syn had gotten his messages. In the meantime, he and his father were going to have a little chat.

Chapter 17

Synthia paced in front of the conference room. Where the hell was Tristan? She checked her watch. He was supposed to be here an hour ago. Thankfully she had access to the presentation materials, so she'd had one of the assistants help her set up his boards.

She'd already checked with Reception and he hadn't called in sick. Hadn't left a message either. Maybe he'd called her cell? She checked the clock. She didn't have time to go back to her office and retrieve it. Okay, then, she was going to do this alone. Fair enough. Presenting she could do in her sleep. It was the whole infusing fun thing she didn't know how to do.

Whatever. She'd fake it till she made it. After everything he'd said about how important this job was to him, how he needed this as validation, she couldn't believe he'd just blown her off like this. Fine, this job was now hers to lose. And there was no way she was losing.

Walking into the presentation room, she gave Bryan a cheerful smile and hoped the smile she gave Bella looked like a friendly gesture and not the baring of teeth it felt like.

Bella's eyes drifted toward the door. "Where is Tristan?"

Syn's stomach sank. Of course Bella was looking for Tristan. He was who she really wanted. *Sorry, lady, you're stuck with me.* She searched for an answer to this question that was both truthful and wouldn't bite her in the butt later. "He sends his apologies, but he's very ill, so he won't be able to present today. I will be presenting his work as well as mine."

Bryan sat up. "I should have been notified. We could have moved the meeting."

Synthia shook her head. "Tristan knows how important Miss Bliss's time is. He didn't want to waste it. I assure you, I'm well prepared and ready to go." She gritted her teeth to ask the next question. "Or would you prefer to wait until Tristan is available?"

Bella's answer surprised her. "No, go ahead. I'd love to hear what you have to say."

Say what? Syn forced a smile. Okay, then. *Showtime.* She turned out the lights and moved the mouse on her laptop to make the screen appear. "Fantastic. If you will draw your eyes to the first slide."

For two hours she presented both her information and Tristan's. She answered all of Bella's questions on pricing and room size as well as financials and areas for improvement and she answered Bryan's questions about amenities, but with every word about the race cars or about the dinner and show, she thought about Tristan. The way he'd laughed and taken her around Vegas. The way he'd looked at her. He couldn't have been faking all that. Could he?

When she was done, Bella leaned back in her seat. "Well, you certainly are thorough. Tristan told me you were the best."

Synthia blinked. Tristan had said that about her? Her heart squeezed. Shoot, she'd gotten it wrong. He hadn't been cozying up to Bella to get the job. Whatever had been going on at the bar, he wasn't trying to hurt her.

Syn forced her mind to go back to Saturday and made herself remember. Bella's hands had been on his face. Bella's body had been pressed flush against his. Where had Tristan's arms been? The memory came into focus. His hands had been on hers. He hadn't been holding her. Her lungs squeezed and she couldn't breathe.

Oh God. She'd lost him. All because she was terrified and didn't want to get hurt.

She had to talk to him. But first she'd have to get through this.

Bella tapped the table with her pen. "I must admit, I'm sorry that Mr. Dawson isn't here, but you did a brilliant job. Please make sure your findings are sent to my office."

What, as if she was some kind of amateur? "Already done."

For once Bella gave her a genuine smile, complete with crinkly eyes. "Of course it is. You certainly think everything through. I especially loved the video elements from the vantage point of the guest. That was brilliant, especially on the helicopter ride and the dash camera on the cars. I felt like I was really taking part. We could use something like that for B-roll in our marketing materials."

That had been Tristan's idea. If Synthia was being honest with herself, her presentation alone would have been dry. Sure, she would have mentioned the amenities and the luxury experiences, but Tristan had taken it a step further. He'd managed to incorporate depth of feeling into the presentation. "Thank you. Tristan spearheaded that effort."

Bella twirled her pen and nodded thoughtfully. "How would you like to be the brand management lead for the Bliss Hotel in Las Vegas?"

Adrenaline pumped through her veins. This was it, what she wanted. What she'd worked so hard for. She'd pulled it off.

But not alone. The presentation wouldn't have been the same without Tristan's input. And it would have been even better if he'd been here to present with her. He would have brought a certain level of enthusiasm. It really didn't kill her to have a little fun, and in this instance, it had upped her game. *Tristan* had upped her game.

Tristan had put in just as much work as she had. And he wanted it just as bad. She couldn't cut him out of the running, could she? He deserved this as much as she did.

She wanted this job…but she wasn't doing this alone. "Under one condition. That Tristan and I share the job. The presentation is half his."

Bella frowned. "But he wasn't here."

"That's the deal. Both of us or none of us."

Bella slid a glance at Bryan, who smirked. "If you're sure that's what you want."

"You two finally realize you're better together?" Bryan asked.

Synthia nodded. "Something like that."

"Great news. Because if you two hadn't worked out your differences, I would have had to find another team."

The moment she left the presentation room, Syn made a beeline for her office. She passed Olivia's office on the way, and her friend followed behind her. "Hey, girl, where's the fire? How did it go? Did Mr. Sex on a Stick really not show?"

Syn grabbed her purse, fishing for her phone. "Yeah, he was a no-show, but I presented his part anyway."

Olivia folded her arms. "I'm getting the impression that you didn't throw him under the bus."

"No. If he isn't here, it means something is wrong." Her hand wrapped around her phone, and relief rushed through her. "Bella gave me the account. I get to work on the branding."

Olivia narrowed her eyes. "This should be happy, booty-dance, in-your-face time. Why is there no in-your-face dancing? I came just for that."

"Because I told Bella that Tristan and I should work together. That it made more sense that way. *And* that we're a team."

Liv's voice went soft. "Sounds like someone got bit by the love bug."

"Yeah, you could say that." Syn played her messages. The first three were from Saturday. But there was one early this morning around six. She hadn't even heard the phone ring. She hit Play.

"Syn, I'm sorry. I won't be there today. My mother is at Santa Barbara General, so I have to go up and see her. There's been an accident. I know you don't trust me, but I'm hoping we can sit down and talk later. Good luck today. I have a feeling you don't need me anyway."

The lump in her throat constricted her airflow. "Oh no, Liv, I screwed up."

"What happened?"

"I took Xia out on Saturday to spend some quality sister time and I saw Tristan with some guy and Bella Bliss was there."

Liv's eyes went round. "As in Bliss Hotels Bella Bliss?"

"Yeah, as in has-been-trying-to-climb-into-Tristan's-pants-since-she-laid-eyes-on-him Bella Bliss. She was wrapped around him in a way that looked like they were about to kiss." She suppressed the flare of rage. "He saw me, I took off. You can guess what happened next."

Liv strode over and wrapped her arms around her. "Oh, Honey Bunches of Oats. You put them walls right back up and he pushed too hard and you pushed too hard, and that was the end of that."

Syn choked out a laugh. "Yeah, pretty much. It's almost like you were there."

Olivia pulled back. "Look, I've said it from the beginning, you two are better when you're together, and from the looks of it, you love him, so I'll cover for you here. Go find him. I'm sure he wants to hear you say you love him."

Syn grabbed her purse. "Okay, I have a call this afternoon with Jefferson Books. Do you think you can take it and if Bryan is looking for me tell him that I went to see Tristan and we're brainstorming and—"

"Would you just go? I got this. And you have a man to go get."

Yes. Yes, she did.

Chapter 18

"Tristan."

The familiar voice had him turning around. It sounded like— "Syn, what are you doing here?"

She reached him and dragged in a deep breath. "I got your call about your mother. Is everything okay?"

She'd come all the way up from LA to check on him? "Um, yeah, she's in traction, but she'll be fine. You didn't have to come all the way up here."

"I know, but I was worried and I knew if you missed the presentation that it was something big. I didn't get your message until after."

He sighed. So she'd thought he'd abandoned her? "I wouldn't just not show."

"I know that. I knew that as soon as you didn't show up. You worked your ass off on this. I know it was important to you. You wouldn't have just vanished."

At least she knew that much about him. "So, how did it go? I assume Bryan was pissed."

She shook her head. "The presentation isn't important right now. How is your mother? How did she end up in traction?"

Tristan sighed. "My old man made it sound more serious than it was to get me down here. He knew the presentation was today. He wanted to exert some of the Dawson power."

She leaned away from him. "Are you kidding me right now?"

He shook his head. "Nope. I really wish I was."

"That's just crazy."

"Yeah, well, you don't know my dad. He doesn't do rebellion very well, so Mom's accident was the perfect reason to pull me away from what I wanted." He shrugged. "It's just how he does things. He sets bombs to everything he touches. I don't think the old man will ever understand that the more he pushes to control me, the more I'll just do my own thing. We had a chance to talk and he's still not behind my choices." He shrugged. "But I think he respects me a little more for standing my ground with him."

Her smile was soft. "Even I've learned that lesson by now."

God, he missed her. What he wanted to do was hold her right now. But he kept his distance. She'd made it clear how she felt about him on Saturday. "I guess you have."

"Tristan, I'm sorry," she blurted out.

"What? About my dad? He's not your fault. I make it a point to thank my grandparents every chance I get."

"No, about Saturday. About all of it. I was scared as hell and seeing you with Bella just gave me a reason to hide. To prove that loving you was a mistake. I should have just listened to you, but I didn't know how."

Loving him? His blood rushed. She'd just said loving him. "Wait, can you repeat that last part?"

A soft smile tugged at her lips. "What? About me not knowing how?"

He tilted his head. "No, before that."

"Oh, you mean, the part about how seeing you with Bella just gave me a reason to hide?"

"Sort of, but the part right after."

She grinned. "Oh, the part about me loving you? Yeah, I'm a little late to the party. I finally figured out that all those feelings that were making me feel insane, that was just the love talking."

"Now you tell me."

"Well, there's something else too. Bella offered me the job today."

He nodded. "I figured she would."

"But I told her the only way I was taking it is if I had a partner."

Warmth started to spread in his chest. "A partner?"

"Yes, because I'm better with you. We need each other. I need you. And I don't want to do it without you. And Bella agrees with me. *We* landed the job."

Tristan grinned as he pulled her to him. "If you can just go back to that part about loving me again and stop there, I'd be the happiest guy in the world."

"I love you, Tristan Dawson."

"And I love you, Synthia Michaels."

"I'm so glad to hear that because you're going to be stuck with me for quite some time."

"Sounds like heaven to me."

* * * * *

I want to thank my fans (the Mynxers) for allowing me
to create from the heart and for proving that romance
should be explored and celebrated beyond color lines.
After six years of growing as an author, I have learned
from and been inspired by some of the best: Erica Rigdon,
Danielle Harden, Kay Young, Natasha Kelly, Reese Dante,
Alicia Spencer, Denise Cherry, Debra Boxton,
Janet Tillman, Simone Harris and so many more.
Because of all of you I have reached a great benchmark
in my writing career. Here's to much more!

Dear Reader,

Who wouldn't love to be stranded on a deserted island with
a man who had the body of a quarterback and the finesse of
Romeo? Could you throw away your inhibitions and give
in to passion with a man who was your sister's husband's
brother? A Casanova with petal-soft lips and muscles made
of concrete, someone whose wealth and famous friends kept
the tabloids celebrating their bachelorhood?

Maybe you could if a midnight boat cruise left you stranded
and alone with him on the most beautiful moonlit beach in
the Caribbean. But what if you discover that the accident
and romance was all part of his plan to possess you? Could
you forgive and separate passion from lust to find your
playboy lover's heart?

I dare you to try to resist. Deja doesn't.

Sienna Mynx

SHIPWRECKED

Sienna Mynx

Prologue

The Wedding

"Hey? Watch where you're going!"

Jon caught the beauty by her arm before their bodies slammed down to the floor. He'd been thoughtless. Too caught up in his own personal discontent and frustrations to be concerned with those who dared to step in his path. But who knew a wrong turn could improve the night considerably?

"Sweetheart, let me help," he said. A bit winded himself, he squeezed her arm to keep her upright. His touch lingered. A natural response to the lovely fragrance she wore and voluptuous curves that he couldn't help but admire. The young woman yanked her arm away and began to wipe at the splatter of champagne across her chest with her drink napkin. Frantic brushes to her purple bridesmaid's dress spread the wet spot around her breasts instead of drying it. Jon couldn't help but notice how her nipples peaked from either the humid outdoor temperature or friction. He observed the jolly movement of her breasts in amusement. A medium-sized pair of beauties exposed thanks to the deep V-neck bodice she wore. She had a trim waistline that complimented her full heart-shaped hips too. The lady possessed the kind of feminine grace that gave a red-blooded man like himself X-ray vision with a vivid imagination.

"Didn't you see me standing here?" she asked. A coppery mix of golden highlights with loose curls that cascaded to her shoulders.

Oh, shit. This wasn't one of the cute bridesmaids he'd collided with. It was the bride's sister. *What was her name? Dejon, Delilah, Darla?* They were introduced only a few hours before the ceremony— why couldn't he recall her name? He'd noticed her the moment they had been paired to walk arm and arm down the aisle. If he hadn't argued with his father earlier that day over something trivial, he might not have dropped his focus and pursued the beauty.

"I should have seen you," he cleared his throat. The action drew her gaze up from the stain on her dress to his eyes. "You're one of the most beautiful women here," he said in a voice unintentionally thick with desire. Her gaze was so cold it pierced him like a spear of ice. Man, he wasn't prepared for those eyes. Long-lashed, deep brown with amber sparks. This lovely beauty had the eye color of his favorite brandy when held under light. The kind of eyes certain to snare a man from a single glance. Her pretty face, with its plump lips and smooth deep brown skin, was the deal sealer. The right side of her hair was tucked behind her ear. She wore large diamond studs that glistened and sparkled from her dainty little lobes, and big bracelets that created their own music each time she moved to wipe at her dress.

"This is going to stain!" she sighed.

He had to chuckle. *Who cares about the dress, doesn't she see me drooling here?* She caught his reaction and his smile deepened at the way her cute little nose wrinkled and her lips pressed together in offense. Finally it looked as if she recognized him. *Who wouldn't?* He was damn near a celebrity in every circle, especially one as personal as his kid brother's wedding.

"I'm Jon Hendrix, Cliff's older brother. Looks like you bumped into me, sweetheart," he teased. It was her turn to apologize. Fawn all over him like the rest of the women at the reception. He arched a brow with expectation.

"Stay in your lane, Jon." She huffed and sashayed off. The swing of her hips, the sway of her locks and the trail of her fragrance as she escaped made her parting even more bitterly received.

His brows lowered and his gaze narrowed over the disrespect. "Did she just dismiss me?" he asked himself.

Jon eyed the other guests laughing and smiling around him, certain someone had seen the snub. Since when did any woman take an immediate dislike to him? *That was new.* He tracked her as she moved through the crowd of guests dancing and gathering around to gush over having not seen each other since the last Hendrix family event. He caught her as she shot him a final glare over her shoulder before disappearing into the mix. *He was definitely losing his touch.*

"What was that about?" his father barked from behind him.

Jon tore his eyes away from the crowd the beauty had slipped through and focused on dear old dad. "Nothing, a misunderstanding. She'll be okay."

His father stared at him for a moment. "That young lady is the bride's sister. You are not to make that family uncomfortable. Are we clear?"

"I don't need a lecture," Jon shot back.

"You will not embarrass the family," his father said through clenched teeth. "Are we clear?" he repeated.

"Right. Clear. I won't break the facade, reveal who we really are," Jon said.

Elvin Hendrix scowled. "You plan on staying for the toast or vanishing yet again?"

"I'm here for Cliff, not you. Of course I intend to stay," Jon answered. He followed his father's gaze. They stood side by side watching his little brother sweep his bride across the dance floor. His parents never ceased to amaze him. They lived very pretentious, exclusive lives. But from the moment his baby brother showed up with his African-American fiancée and announced he would marry her, his family had been nothing but accepting. He had to wonder, if he had made the same choice in a woman, would his father have been so tolerant?

"He's done well. Look at them." His father said with a proud smile. "They're perfect."

Jon rolled his eyes. "On second thought I need some air. You make the toast."

Before his father could respond he started off. The crowd at the open bar was too congested for him to quickly grab a bottle so he turned left. There was a bar inside the hotel. Forget the wedding. Forget dear ole dad and his judgment. He'd grab a few bottles and catch the last of the game.

"I'm done!" Deja announced.

"Done? Dee hasn't thrown the bouquet. She hasn't

danced with Daddy yet. Whoa…wait, what happened to your dress?"

"That jerk over there walked directly into me. Spilled my champagne." Deja pointed to the shifting crowd of guests clustered near the buffet table. There were too many people gathered around, but none of them she knew. The lawns to the back of the resort hotel were vast and as green as emeralds. The Hendrix family owned the grounds as they did many others. They had insisted their son's wedding and reception both be held in the gardens. Large white tents shielded the guests from the afternoon California sun.

"Who? Who was it?" Dina asked.

Dina was the middle child, and Deja the oldest. That made the bride, their sister, the baby of the trio.

"It was the best man. Now hand over the keys."

"Wait? Jon Hendrix? *The* Jon Hendrix?" Dina asked. She rose on her toes in search of him. "Did you look at the man when you walked down the aisle holding his arm?"

"Why?" Deja asked with disgust.

"Because he's the fine one. The rich one! The only single man here worth a damn, Deja. The man looks like he stepped out of a *GQ* photo shoot. Where is he? Where did he go?"

"Put your tongue back in your mouth before your husband sees. I couldn't care less who he is," Deja said with a sigh.

Dina continued as if she hadn't heard Deja's direction. She walked on her toes to try to locate Jon Hendrix herself. But there were too many guests. "Darn it. He's gone. Deja! Girl, you're missing out. He's the hottest bachelor in the universe. I think he dates black women, too, like his brother. Saw him in a magazine with Layla Thomas."

"I don't care!" Deja scoffed.

"Your last boyfriend was a Cambodian musician. You date the rainbow," Dina snickered. "Don't pretend you aren't interested."

Deja rolled her eyes. "Jackasses come in all races, sister dear. And would you stop pointing out race, Dina, it's embarrassing. What if one of the guests hears you?"

"Oh, please. As if these white folks aren't already scratching their heads over our chocolate little Dee-Dee marrying into this family," Dina said, chuckling.

Deja glanced around to see if anyone had overheard their conversation. Dina had been making digs at Deja's taste in men since their baby sister had come home with a white investment broker who happened to be the youngest male heir to the Hendrix hotel and resort fortune. It wasn't Deja who'd introduced them. They lived in a progressive age. Many people in the bay area dated interracially. But she didn't bother explaining that to her sister. She couldn't care less about the eldest playboy Hendrix.

"Oh, and Darren said he's Robbie Steven's manager," Dina prattled on. "He just signed that kid who won the top college athletic award and signed a deal with one of the best teams in the league. It's all over the news." Dina grinned. "What if he brought Robbie to the wedding? Jeez, Darren would flip out if he got to meet Robbie. Speaking of Darren, have you seen my hubby?"

"No." Deja turned her head and glanced back at the hotel. She should have kept her purse with her.

"Would you stop being such a buzzkill," Dina whispered. "People are already calling you the mean sister."

Startled by the accusation Deja glared at her sister. Dina stepped closer and lowered her voice. "You should be interested that a single cute man is in the vicinity," she said. "Not because he's white. Not because it's been six months since your last date. You should be interested because it's time to move on. I'm married. Dee is married. Look at you. When are you going to stop being such an ice queen and get a little excited about any man again?"

Deja shook her head and stalked off. Dina called her name but she ignored her, picking up her pace. She stepped out from under the tented reception area into the grass. The resort loomed up the hill. When she glanced back she saw her baby sister, Dee, take to the dance floor with her new husband. She paused. Dee looked so happy. She beamed up at her husband who had swept into her life and proposed only a few months later. Her sister deserved happiness. She smiled briefly and started up the hill careful of her sinking shoes in the grass. She'd find her purse and go back to her room. She had an early flight to catch for an interview she had that next week. If it all panned out and she got the teaching gig at NYU she'd start over in New York. Dina was wrong. She didn't need a man. She needed a new beginning.

"Hold the elevator!" A deep voice called out.

Deja hit the button to stop the doors from closing before she identified who had just bolted inside. She should have looked up first. As soon as the doors closed her heart skipped a beat in her chest. He was with her. Jon Hendrix.

"Six please," he said with a hint of a smile.

She tried to appear unaffected by his presence. She pressed the button and lifted her gaze to the electronic number display praying for a swift ride up to the fourth floor. But she could feel him staring. The man's gaze had heat to it. And his presence carried a sense of mystery. Addictive predatory mystery like the bad-boy musicians she loved to bed. But Jon Hendrix was no musician. She peeked at him. He had a pale gold tanned face with coal-black hair and firm chiseled features. A tall athletic frame tucked nicely in a tuxedo. He caught her staring and his piercing blue-gray eyes went smoky dark in an instant and snared her.

"Ah hello," she said.

He gave her a single nod. It was his eyes that did the speaking for him. They swept her face and lowered from her face to her breasts and then her hips. When they returned they sparkled with interest. She swung her gaze back to the number display.

"About earlier, beautiful…" he began.

"Forget about it—" She waved the explanation off and the elevator froze with a jolt. Deja stepped back in surprise. They were on floor three. She pressed the button. Nothing. She hit it with her fist. Nothing. Panic rose like a black tide and dragged her under.

"Hey, it's okay." She heard him say.

She didn't know her emotional collapse was that transparent. She was barely aware that a startled cry of terror had escaped her mouth or that she was panting hard. Immediately she began to breathe hard through her nose, and perspire. Her little secret, unknown even to friends and family, was her claustrophobia. She battled anxiety in small cars, windowless rooms, and yes, elevators.

"We're trapped!" she wheezed.

She looked up into the mirrored wall of the elevator and saw his concern. He must be thinking she was crazy. She felt crazy. "I can't. I can't be stuck in here! It's stuck! It's stuck!" She screamed out loud.

He put a hand to her arm. Deja backed up to the wall with closed eyes. There was constriction in her chest and lungs. A sharp cramp in her gut robbed her of the ability to breathe. She suppressed the urge to cry. "Get me out of here! Get me out!"

"Mr. Hendrix. We will have the elevator moving in a

few minutes, sir. We see you." A man spoke on the intercom.

"Make it quick!" he barked the order.

She opened her eyes and he was in front of her. The look of concern in his smoldering eyes was genuine. "You're okay. Breathe, breathe with me," he said.

"I can't! I can't!" she gasped.

He touched her face. It was the most calming touch she had ever felt. With her back against the elevator wall she felt it all at once. At the base of her spine a hot, white current of terror soothed by a pool of soft, warm sensations. His touch resonated through the bloodstream and she calmed into a warm fuzziness as her heart beat slowed.

"Now. Look at me, look at me, beautiful," he said. "Breathe through your nose and out of your mouth. Inhale deep and exhale slow."

Deja lifted her gaze and looked into his eyes. She did as he instructed. The bubble of hysteria popped. Everything stabilized. She inhaled deep and exhaled slowly through her pursed lips. The color and texture of her surroundings were solid and formed. She had to wonder if it was some kind of aneurysm or brain spasm that brought her collapse on. Surely an intelligent woman like her didn't fall apart because of a stuck elevator.

He smiled. "Wow, sweetheart. Are you always this intense?" he asked.

Instead of being insulted she actually appreciated his humor. She just couldn't speak just yet. Instead, she smiled and kept breathing.

"Good girl. Feel better?" he asked.

She nodded.

"I'm sorry," she croaked. "It's just not my day, or year for that matter."

When he stepped closer she touched his chest. It was

a reflex reaction and a strong one. The hard strength she felt underneath the fine silk threads of his shirt vibrated through her palm. She relaxed. She was scared, but not panicked as she once was. "How…how long before… before the doors open?"

"Minutes. These things happen." He looked up at the ceiling and then back down to her. "Probably a circuit of some sort. He'll get us out of here."

"I can't stay in here," Deja pleaded. "I really can't." She closed her eyes and swallowed. She tried not to think of the suffocation rising in her lungs once more. "I… I have anxiety."

"Hey, do you know the truth about anxiety?" he asked as he lifted her chin.

She blinked up at him. "What truth?"

"Nothing lasts, beautiful. Not the feeling of happiness, of sadness, fear, even anxiety. You can't feel the same emotion consistently forever. So if you focus on me for the next several minutes, you'll be out before the terror returns."

Was he for real? She stared into his eyes. His boldly handsome face held a certain sensuality. His hair gleamed under the bright elevator lights with dark tendrils curled at the edge of his forehead. His eyes, chiseled features and self-confident presence gave him a larger-than-life appearance. All he needed was the square rimmed glasses and he'd be a super hero in disguise. The man crowded her with his height. He had her blocked in against the wall. He began to touch her wherever he pleased from her face, arms to her hips. She could only look to him for help. And something mischievous sparked in his eyes that said that was his intention. Plus he was tall. The man was so stunningly virile she lost all fear of confinement. Deja was a sucker for tall men. Her tastes tended to lean more toward the lanky guitarist in rock bands, with a penchant for leather pants and heartbreaks. But a jet-setting celebrity playboy could fit the bill.

"Looks like you're feeling better. Right?" he asked.

"You sound like a shrink," she tried to joke.

"Seen a few," he winked.

Deja chuckled. She prayed he would continue to speak and touch her, distract her. And her prayers were answered. Except this time his hands were stroking up and down her arms. And he was closer. So close she could feel his body heat.

"What's your name?" he asked. His hand moved to hers and squeezed.

"Huh?" she answered.

"Your name is huh?" he asked.

She laughed and shook her head no.

"Tell me your name, beautiful," he said. They'd met just an hour before the wedding. He'd walked her down the aisle. Didn't he remember? When she considered it further, she recalled that besides the drink spill incident they hadn't spoken, and were never formally introduced.

"Your name?" he whispered again. God help her, her knees nearly gave way. All he was doing was stroking her arm and it excited her.

"Deja," she said.

"Ah, Deja. Very beautiful."

She was about to request some space. She desperately needed him to give her at least ten inches for air and sanity. The elevator, however, shook and dropped a floor. Deja screamed. She leaped at him and he scooped her up into his arms fully. His strong embrace crushed her against a solid chest. She deliberately shut out awareness of how nice it was to be pressed against him.

It didn't work.

The kiss happened.

And it felt right.

Deja kissed him. His tongue swept in her mouth and she gripped the nape of his neck as a slender delicate thread of desire wrapped around them. Her insides jangled with excitement and her body bloomed with lust so thick and languid it threatened to take them under. Oh, yes, she welcomed this drowning.

Passion greeted him where he expected resistance. The heat of her mouth, the tangled dance of their tongues, the woman herself made his loins burn. Nothing prepared him for how soft and beautiful she would feel to him after one single kiss.

His hand began to slip ever so slowly around her slender waist and then down to cup her round ass. And she held on to him. He squeezed her butt with both hands and elicited a shudder from her, which his ego absorbed and savored. Strange, but ever since he bumped into the lovely Deja he'd wanted to feel her ass. It was nicely formed in her bridesmaid's dress. He wished to buy her a closet full of those dresses.

The elevator shook again as if trying to make a climb. The lights inside blinked off. She whimpered and he felt her body's tremble go through him.

"I have you," he whispered between the kiss and licks of her lips before he kissed her harder. He took her into his arms. He pushed her up against the elevator wall to prevent her escape. He wanted her undivided attention. The bulge of his erection was now pressed against the apex of her sex. He found her petal-soft and warm between her thick thighs and wondered if she was tight for him, as well. She groaned. The elevator responded with a loud grinding of gears. As if a switch was flipped it came to life and started to climb.

The doors opened just as her legs parted and her dress inched up further.

"Ahem. Mr. Hendrix, sir?"

She tore her mouth from his and pushed against his chest. But he wanted more. Infuriated, he glanced back to see Pedro, the maintenance guy, staring in at them.

"Excuse me," Deja said as she escaped him. He tried to go after her but Pedro got in the way. When he did make it into the hall she was at her room door with her key card. And in a flash she was gone.

"Everything okay?" Pedro asked.

"Back off!" he snarled.

The man blinked, shocked, and turned away. Jon touched his lips. Never in his life had he burned as much with the need for more.

Chapter 1

The Anniversary, Two Years Later

"Miss? Miss?"

Deja blinked awake. The flight attendant smiled down at her. It was a nice warm smile from a red-haired lady in her midthirties with green eyes. "I need you to bring your seat up and fasten your seat belt. We're about to land. Thank you."

"Oh? Okay," Deja felt her cheeks burn hot with embarrassment. She hoped she hadn't been snoring. She brought her seat upright. The passenger next to her smiled. He was an older man who had told her he was on his way to the island to meet up with his daughter and wife for vacation. She nodded to the man and turned her gaze to the window. Below she could see the deep blue waters of the Pacific.

Ladies and gentlemen, this is your captain speaking.

We are making our approach to the Abaco Islands and would like to ask that you remain in your seats for the remainder of the flight. The temperature today in Abaco is a lovely 77 degrees. Welcome to paradise.

The intercom clicked off. Deja sighed. The word paradise swirled in her mind. She needed this vacation. She couldn't remember the last time she'd taken one. As she stared at the islands' lush green trees and white beaches upon their approach, her memory conjured the dream she'd had just moments ago. Two years later, and the kiss in the elevator by the world's most talked-about and photographed bachelor still made her heart race.

She had only seen Jon Hendrix twice since, at family functions hosted by her sister. Both times she'd shied away from any contact or conversation with the man. But she'd caught his stares from across the room. Now she was joining her sister and the Hendrix family for their second anniversary. This one was special because Dee was pregnant. The first baby to be had between the sisters and even her father was overjoyed at the thought of the little boy who would soon join their family.

Deja put on her sunglasses. The wheels of the plane bounced on the paved runway and then the aircraft braked hard, causing all the passengers to jostle in their seats. She exhaled.

"Welcome to paradise," she mumbled.

"Jon!"

Someone kicked the back of his chair and his feet crashed from the coffee table to the floor. He shot up alert and awake. The sunglasses shielding his bloodshot eyes from the sun dropped to his chin.

"What the hell is your problem?" He adjusted his sunglasses and turned his head slightly to acknowledge his kid brother.

"I need you to go to the airport and pick up—"

"No!" Jon answered. He slumped down in his chair and recrossed his legs at the ankles. It wasn't his baby brother's fault that he was hungover and existing on less than twenty-nine minutes of sleep. The celebration for the star NBA player under Jon's management company was a four-day hard-drinking party in Miami Beach. Why he even thought he could come to the islands and coast through this anniversary event was beyond him. Well, he knew why. It was her. He'd jumped at the chance to see her. Though he doubted she'd give him a single hello.

"What I was going to say is can you go to the airport to pick up Deanna's sister. Deja just landed."

Jon sat upright. "Deja?"

"Got your attention, huh?"

"What? No. I mean I barely know her."

His brother pulled out the chair next to him. "Mom is worried about you. Dad and she both think...well, they think you need to slow down. Every time they turn on the news you're out there doing whatever it is you do."

"Not this again. I won't hear it from the old man and I'm not going to listen to it from you."

His brother heaved a deep sigh. "They think you're a self-centered bastard with no focus."

Jon arched a brow, amused.

"Dad thinks you have a drinking or drug habit."

"Is that so, baby brother? And what do you think?" Jon asked.

"I think you're a brilliant businessman. I think it takes more than fancy clothes and fast women to manage some of the world's top athletes. They don't give you enough credit."

Jon snorted. "They never have."

His brother leaned forward. "The problem is you give them no reason to. You need to slow down. And I know you got a thing for Deanna's older sister."

Jon's gaze glided left under the cover of his sunglasses. "I told you I don't know her."

"Hmm...well, do me a favor. Go pick her up. Make her feel welcome." His brother stood.

"Cliff. Wait." Jon sighed. "I'm not an alcoholic and I don't do drugs. But...well, Dad is right. I can't keep going at this pace. I need to slow down. Been thinking of it a lot lately. The company is doing good. I got plenty of contracts and agents on the ground. Maybe I should shift my focus."

"Shift it, huh?" Cliff smiled. "You got someone in mind?"

Jon shrugged. "What time did you say her plane landed?"

"Who?" Cliff chuckled.

Jon punched him in the arm. Cliff winced. He shook his head, smiling.

"She just landed," Cliff smiled.

"I'll pick her up. Needed a break anyway."

Deja struggled. She yanked hard on the handle of her carry-on luggage and dragged her larger suitcase with the other hand through the doors of the airport. The wheels squeaked and she glanced around, embarrassed that she was too cheap to invest in something more modern and convenient. But that was how she managed everything in her life. The hard-earned way. She strolled out into the muggy heat of the island and surveyed the cab drivers. Her sister had said she would meet her. She missed Dee.

Her other sister, Dina, and her husband, Darren, couldn't make it to the island because of their work schedules.

Deja frowned. "Where is she?"

"Deja!" She heard her name being called. She turned and saw a man approaching fast. She wanted to run. It was him. Jon wore khaki cargo pants and a crisp white shirt. He looked tan, tall and yummy. Damn it! She had told Dee specifically that she didn't want to be paired with him. Why was he there?

"Hi?" he said.

"Hi," she managed to smile.

"May I?" he asked.

"Oh, uh, sure," she said as she let go of the handle to her luggage. He dragged it with ease.

"My car is just over there. How was your flight?" he asked as he walked and stared at her. Deja sucked down a confident breath. She kept up with him and managed to appear calm.

"Long. Had a layover in Miami. Glad to be upright and walking in sunshine," she joked.

"I understand. Have you ever been to Abaco?" he asked her.

"No. Never. Deanna said your family owns a part of the island. Is that true?" she asked. He stepped off the curb. She stood by the car watching him. She had to admit she loved the sight of his muscled arms as he lifted her luggage and placed it in the trunk of the car.

"We own quite a bit of land but not the island or the politics. We also own a few of the smaller islands off the coast. You'll have a great time." He slammed the trunk down and stepped around her. He opened the passenger-side door. "I plan to see to it," he said.

Deja wasn't sure how to respond. The teasing smile on his lips was sexy. But she couldn't see his eyes behind the dark lenses of his sunglasses. You could always tell a person's intentions by their eyes. So instead of commenting she eased inside the car and he closed the door behind her.

You can do this. Play it cool. He's like family or something. And the kiss was two years ago. The man has definitely moved on. She knew that for a fact. Thanks to social media, tabloid blogs and websites, she had unlimited access into Jon Hendrix's life. The bachelor lifestyle he led was broadcasted constantly on the pages of every media outlet. From the movie-star dates and the flashy parties with sports figures. He was just as well-known as his clients.

"Buckle up! I want to get you there safely," he said, smiling.

Deja hadn't realized her seat belt wasn't buckled. She fastened it across her chest while he observed her. He didn't start the car until she was done. It was going to be a long ride.

Jon fought against his own urges and kept his eyes trained on the road. He sensed that he made her uncomfortable. And the bastard in him secretly enjoyed her uneasiness. She had snubbed him twice since their elevator kiss. It was as if she looked right through him. As if she didn't feel what he had felt between them in that elevator. Now she stared straight ahead silently, with her hands clasped in her lap as if unable to make conversation. Deja felt the attraction. He knew it. He shook his head, smiling.

"Music?" he asked. Maybe some island tunes would calm her and make her feel less pressured to communicate with him.

"Yes, please," she agreed.

He found a calypso station and they coasted out of the city into the mango groves. She gripped the inside of the door twice. But he caught the way her head rocked slightly in time with the rhythmic beat.

Deja was lovelier than he remembered her. She'd cut her hair. And she had done something else to it. It was more crinkly than curly. It had a puffy flair to it. He considered it a nice style that revealed more of her natural beauty. She wore wooden hoop earrings and wooden bracelets on her right arm to match. Her yellow summer dress was strapless but her short-sleeve sweater was closed to cover her bosom. However, he had a good memory. He recalled how thick and soft her thighs were and the warmth he'd felt when her breasts were mashed against his chest. He remembered everything.

"To hell with this," he mumbled under his breath, so low she didn't hear him. He turned the radio off.

She shot him a curious look. Her sunglasses were in her hair so he could see her long-lashed brown eyes.

"Why don't you like me?" he asked.

"What?" she asked.

"Me? Why don't you like me?" he asked again.

"I don't know what you mean." she looked away.

"Oh, come on. You gave me the hottest kiss I've ever had and have treated me like I was invisible since. Did I do something to offend you?"

"Could we not talk about the kiss," she said, sighing.

"Ah, no. I want to talk about the kiss. Damn. I want another one," he challenged her.

This time her gaze slipped to him under lowered lashes. "Well, that's not going to happen. The kiss was a mistake, okay? I don't know you enough not to like you. I just wanted to avoid the awkwardness."

"Didn't feel awkward to me when you were in my arms."

"Oh, my God! Enough already! I'm sure you have hundreds of girls to give you a kiss."

Jon steadied his driving. Her comment stung. "What does that mean? I have a hundred girls?"

"Forget it. Never mind. It's none of my business who you sleep with."

"Let's be clear, sweetheart. I don't collect women or have them on speed dial. No matter what you have heard from my brother!" he snapped.

"Are you kidding? Do you think I'm an idiot?" she sassed him. "I can't turn on the computer or pick up a magazine without seeing you with some movie star or big-breasted blonde trophy!"

Her remark hit him hard. He nearly swerved out of the lane. He sped along the winding road that inched closer to his family's resort, with his hands tightly gripping the steering wheel. When he spoke he did so through clenched teeth. "That's bullshit! That's my business, not my life!"

"Whatever," she rolled her eyes. "Looks like one and the same to me."

She was busting his balls with a hammer now. He'd had enough. He hated having to explain himself. So what if he loved women and dated many? It had nothing to do with their kiss. But at least he had his answer. The truth was living the fast life had left him quite lonely. Every woman he enjoyed had left or was eventually pushed away by his restlessness. He wouldn't bother telling her that. Forget it. He owed no one an explanation on his life.

The drive to the resort was shortened by his speed. He delivered her within minutes. Before she could offer an apology for her attitude, he had hopped out the car and was headed to the back of it. Jon had a problem with his anger. This he knew. Whenever he felt it swell in his chest and stun his breathing he did his best to escape the situation. He removed her luggage and pushed it over to her.

"Enjoy your stay," he remarked and walked off. He didn't look back.

Deja blinked. It was ironic, really. She'd spent half her flight thinking about the kiss they'd shared. But the moment he mentioned it, she'd attacked the man. Arguing with Jon Hendrix was frustrating but being dismissed by him disappointed her more. He stalked off to the left instead of up the stairs to the resort entrance. Chivalry was dead and Casanova was done. He probably wouldn't say any more than the parting words he had left her with for the remainder of her visit.

"Damn it, Deja. You and your mouth."

"Good evening, ma'am, welcome. Let me be of assistance," a short dark-skinned man in a flowered resort short and white slack pants greeted her. He took hold of her luggage immediately. She smiled and started toward the resort. She wanted to find her sister first thing. However, when they entered she was steered toward the check-in.

"Welcome to the Oasis. Your luggage will be taken upstairs. The guests are expected to gather on the verandah in one hour for the festivities. Here is your room key."

She accepted the key card and gift bag. "Festivities?" Deja asked.

"Oh, yes. We have a great time planned for all of you, including night sailing."

Deja swallowed. No way in hell she wanted to get on a boat at night. "My sister. I want to see her. What is her room number?"

"She's in our Commander Suite. Room 3200. I can ring her and let her know that you are here."

"That won't be necessary. I can find my way. I'd rather surprise her," she said, then slid the key card into her purse.

Jon Hendrix was nowhere to be seen. It was just as well. They really didn't need the embarrassment of another awkward moment between them.

When she arrived on the top floor to the Oasis she found the Commander Suite was the only door to knock on. She knew Dee lived well. Much better than Deja could afford, with her salary as a college professor. The extravagance and exclusivity of her baby sister's life worried her. The three of them were drifting apart.

She knocked. No answer. She saw a buzzer next to the door and pressed it.

"Yes?" a familiar voice called out of the speaker system.

"Dee? It's me! Deja!" she answered.

"Come in!" her sister said.

A buzzing noise preceded the lock's disengagement and Deja opened the door without the need of a key card. She stepped inside.

"Back here! In the bedroom!" she heard her sister yell.

The space was very open. The windows gave a panoramic view of the sea. Startled by the beauty of the ocean she stared for a moment at the sapphire-blue waters with white sailboats anchored underneath a clear sky.

"Deja? I'm in here!" Her sister called for her.

She started off in the direction of her sister's voice and found her room. Dee grinned from the bed. She stretched out her arms for a hug. She was huge. Seven months pregnant and swollen in the face, hands and feet. Deja's heart expanded at the sight of her. She hurried over and kissed and hugged her sister.

"I've been waiting all day for you. So excited! I've missed you so much!" Dee gushed.

"Baby, why are you in bed? Is something wrong?" Deja asked, checking her over.

Dee waved off the concern. "My blood pressure. I have a private doctor here. He said I can't do the sailing tonight. I have to stay in bed as much as possible," she said with a pout. "But I'll be at the pre-party to send you off."

"Sailing? Blood pressure?" Deja glanced around the room. "Where's Cliff?"

"Oh, he's around. So did Jon pick you up from the airport?" Dee asked.

Deja's gaze swung back around to her kid sister. She could see the light of mischief sparkling in her eyes. "Did you send him?"

Dee grinned.

"Why?"

"You know why," Dee teased.

Deja crossed her arms over her chest. "Enlighten me."

All these months and neither one of her sisters had ever commented on the incident at the wedding. She had only shared the experience with Dina. Now she suspected Dina had spilled the secret liaison and they were now conspiring against her. Trying to fix her up.

"Answer me, Dee!" Deja insisted.

"Oh, don't get pissy," Dee said. "Dina told me that you kissed him on the day of the wedding."

"I knew it!" Deja felt her gut clench.

"So what? A kiss. It was just a kiss, Deja. And Jon is constantly asking about you so it must have been good. Right? Is that why you make a point to ignore the poor guy whenever he comes into a room? Never mind. We decided to help you out."

"Help me?" Deja asked.

Dee grinned.

"Why can't you two mind your own damn business?" Deja asked. "That would be a great help."

"Calm down! Dina and I thought it might be cool if you came to the island and got a chance to loosen up. Have some fun. They say a lot of things about Jon but boring isn't one of them."

"It's not cool." Deja let her exasperation show. "And with him of all people."

"Jon is a nice guy. If you give him a chance you might find out you like him."

"The man is a wolf. He sleeps with hundreds of women. Lives that life. C'mon, Dee, you know what kind of jerk he is. You said it yourself before you married into this family!"

"I was wrong. I judged him before I met him. Like you're currently doing. Talk to him. See for yourself. He's harmless."

"Okay, let's stop." Deja sat on the edge of the bed. "Forget the dating game. I haven't seen you in so long."

Dee smiled. "We Skype all the time."

"Not the same and you know it." Deja chuckled. "Sorry I missed the baby shower. Tell me what's going on with you. Why is your blood pressure high?" She put her hand on her kid sister's stomach. Tears glistened in her sister's eyes.

"I'm going to be a mother. Can you believe it?" Dee asked.

"I'm so happy for you," Deja nodded.

"They said I couldn't overdo it. The last trimester the baby is growing fast. I need to slow down and take it easy.

Cliff is worried. That's why we are sharing our second anniversary with friends and family. He thinks it will be calming to have you here."

"Will it be?" Deja asked.

"This island calms me. I'm too happy for stress. But I can understand my husband's fears. I don't need him having anxiety attacks over my dance moves."

The sisters shared a laugh.

"I wish Dina could have come," Deja said through her smile. "I told her I'd pay for it. But she said no."

Deja touched her sister's cheek. "Dina had to work. I'm here and Daddy arrives tomorrow. That's all we need."

"Mama? Have you spoken to her?" Dee asked with a ring of hope in her voice.

Their mother had been estranged from them in the past few years since the divorce. She didn't come to the wedding, and she barely returned any of their calls. She thought her mom was punishing them for siding with their father during the divorce. Ironically it was dear old mom who would miss out on the most precious changes in her daughters' lives. "Let's not worry about Ma. We got some celebrating to do."

Dee grinned. "You have to get changed. Wear something cute."

"This is cute." Deja stood and spun in her yellow summer dress.

Dee arched a brow. "Okay, not cute. Wear something sexy. A bikini."

"Please, I'm not going to dinner in a bikini," Deja laughed.

"Everyone is. And let's face it, Deja, you got the best damn body of us three. Tonight is going to be so beautiful. We own a private island not far from here. We have it all planned. Music, a man eating fire, and lanterns to light up the entire beach so we can dance and swim under the moon. I'm so excited!" she clapped.

"I thought you weren't coming?"

"Well, I'm still working on that," Dee winked.

Deja looked her sister over. Dee was positively glowing with beauty and happiness. "The things I do for you," Deja said with a chuckle.

"Go on! Get dressed! Shoo!" Dee said.

Shaking her head and blowing a kiss from her hand, Deja left.

Jon popped the twist cap off the bottle of ginger beer and drank it down. He dropped onto a wicker chair underneath the lazy blades of a large ceiling fan. The outdoor decks to the back of the resort faced the sea and a few tourists were out enjoying the day. He had intended to drift off to sleep on top of his favorite hammock under one of the palms but this was as far as he got. Jon took another long swig of the cool ginger beer.

"Something wrong?" his brother asked.

He didn't bother to look up. He had overreacted. He knew it and it was too late to undo it. Deja must really think him a jackass.

"Did you pick up Dee's sister from the airport?" Cliff asked.

Jon closed his eyes.

His brother cast a cool look back at him from over his shoulder. "I asked you a question. Did you bring her?"

"You know I did." Jon sighed. He drank down the last of his beer and sat upright. He looked over to Cliff. "Got a question for you, little brother."

"I don't have any time for games, Jon."

"It's a simple question." Jon waited a beat. His brother stared at him expectantly. "What keeps you up at night?"

His brother turned to fully face him. He rested on the balcony with his back to the ocean wind and swaying palms. "The thought of anything going wrong with Dee and the baby when she goes into labor. That's what keeps me up at night."

Jon nodded. "Want to know what keeps me up at night?"

His brother blinked and then gave him a single nod.

"That maybe Dad is right about me. Maybe what everybody thinks of me is who I am."

"You care what people think?" Cliff asked.

"People? Hell, no. Dad? You? I pretend I don't. Pretty good at it, too." Jon chuckled. "But yeah. I guess I do."

Before Cliff could respond with one of his generic pep talks Jon stood. He shook his head and walked off.

Chapter 2

Sailing

A fresh shower made all the difference. Jon walked out of the resort lobby to where everyone had gathered. The calypso band led the way. He inhaled the sweet fragrance of the evening wind blowing in from the sea and the tropical flowers that bloomed on every branch. With his hands in his pockets and his eyes hidden behind his sunglasses he had arrived almost in time for the dinner announcement in progress.

"So again, thank you all for coming. Celebrating my marriage to the most special woman in the world." Cliff kissed Dee and then kissed her swollen tummy. Most of those gathered cheered. Dee laughed and rubbed the top of her husband's head. He then continued with his speech. "This evening we sail at sunset. It's the most beautiful time on the island. Our island is just three miles off the coast. We will take my yacht and you will all be swept up in paradise. Join us tonight as we celebrate the day that changed our lives forever!" He raised his glass.

The guests raised their glasses in salute to the toast. And Cliff kissed his wife. Jon had seen enough. He searched the smiling faces for the one person he intended to spend time with that evening. He found her. She sat at a table with friends of his parents. She clapped and chatted easily with the elderly couple. Deja, too, had changed. She wore a turquoise sarong that tied sexily just above her bosom. He couldn't see much more. Her hair was smoothed back from her face and pinned neatly to the back of her head. Large white feather earrings dropped from her lobes. She glanced his way. When her eyes landed on him they didn't shift away. Those damn eyes of hers. That was the beginning. The spark that had made him touch her in the elevator and want to again. He didn't read the same disapproval he'd seen earlier in her stare and he seized the moment. He was an ass and he intended to say so.

Jon made his way to the table. People began to rise from theirs. Many swarmed the couple with cheer and congratulations for the new addition to the Hendrix family. To his relief the couple that were with Deja did so, as well. She was alone by the time he reached her. "May I?" he asked.

She nodded but didn't speak.

The words stuck on her throat and she could barely utter a sound. She'd been waiting to see him again. She'd rehearsed her apology in her head several times. He had changed into another white linen shirt but this time he wore blue shorts that stopped at his knees. The open buttons to the front of his shirt revealed the muscular length of his neck and chest. Kissed by the sun, the man's skin appeared tanned all over. She had to swallow to be sure she wasn't drooling.

"I owe you an apology," he began.

Damn right he did! She gave him a pleasant smile but didn't respond.

He removed his sunglasses and dropped them in his front pocket. Now she could see his bedroom eyes. They peered down at her under long dark lashes. She still couldn't determine if they were blue or gray. His dark hair and light eyes were a striking contrast. His mouth took on a sensuous curve. Could the man read her thoughts, she wondered. His charm revealed more about him than any of the blog sites and magazines ever did. This was Jon Hendrix being sincere. And it was a real turn-on.

"Earlier, you simply stated your opinion and I was rude to you. Guess you hit a nerve. I know what most people think about me. And some of it is true. But that kiss we shared, sweetheart? That was unforgettable. I've been trying to have a conversation with you ever since."

Deja reached for her glass of water. She took a sip of the cool liquid and swallowed. The knot that blocked speech in her throat cleared. She flashed him a polite smile. "I apologize, too. The kiss was…" She glanced away because the firepower in his gaze was just too intense. "Nice. But it was just a kiss, Jon. It happened two years ago…"

"On this very day—" he interjected.

She returned her gaze to him. "We should let it go."

"Agreed. Friends?" he asked and extended his hand.

She glanced to his hand and then up to his smile. After a brief pause she accepted his hand and shook it in return firmly.

"Got an idea," he said and glanced back to the others.

She looked up and saw several of the guests leaving to head toward the yacht. Her sister was laughing merrily with her husband guiding her steps.

"Sail with me tonight."

"I intend to," she said. "In fact we should be going now."

She made to rise but he grabbed her hand. "I have my own boat. We can go for a spin and then head to the island. A short spin," he winked.

Deja bit down on her bottom lip. Her skin grew hot and feverish under his touch. She hadn't allowed herself to encourage the desires she'd suppressed for months. Dating in New York had been one disaster after another. She was done with fickle men and their trivial pursuits.

"What trouble could we get into on the ocean?" he asked.

She laughed. "Seriously?"

"Yes. I want to sail with you. Talk. Get to know you. Hell, we're family, right?" he asked.

"True. Brother and sister," she winked.

"I wouldn't go that far. More like brother-in-law and sister-in-law, or whatever. Yeah, forget the family remark." He wrinkled his nose. Deja laughed again.

"Damn," he said smiling.

"What?" she asked and her hands connected to her waist. She gave him a playful smirk.

"No offense, sweetheart, but I'm surprised. I had no idea you had such a pretty laugh."

"Is that so? You thought my laugh was ugly?"

"No," he said and his gaze swept down. She realized that when she put her hands to her hips it had parted her sarong and he could see her bikini. Deja sucked in a breath to make sure her tummy was tight and allowed him the pleasure. Why not? Dee was right about her body. She had worked hard to maintain her figure. Sure she was full in the hips and ass, but that was all natural, as well as her breasts. She lacked no self-confidence in her physical appearance.

Jon cleared his throat. He then licked and drew in his bottom lip. He dragged his gaze up from the tiny strawberry tattoo just above her bikini line to her face. "It's the first time you've ever laughed around me."

Deja paused. He was right. Since she met him she'd given him a smile or two but not a genuine laugh. "Damn is right. This is the first time you've given me a reason to."

He nodded. "Let me give you another."

He stood and her gaze kept climbing as he did. His height alone could convince her of anything. "Okay," she agreed.

He dropped his head as if in relief. "The woman said yes!"

Deja laughed again. What kind of trouble could they get into on a boat? He'd be more focused on showing off than kissing her. Though secretly she hoped he'd try.

He walked around and extended his arm to her. Deja eased her arm into his.

Jon wasn't prepared for what was under the sarong. When she stood his manhood jumped in his shorts. It was the sexiest white bikini he'd seen a woman's curves tucked into. And he'd seen plenty. The sarong was long. It drifted to her feet and pooled behind her. But when she walked it opened and her legs were revealed. And she didn't shy away from the unveiling. That was the difference between girls and women. Deja had to be in her midthirties. Other than the panic attack in the elevator she had a certain confidence about herself that he didn't see in the young babes who shared his bed. He appreciated her direct manner. When she allowed him to walk her out from under the terrace, he dropped his gaze over to look at her once more. She glanced up at him and he shook his head again while smiling.

"My boat's over there," he said.

She nodded. She glanced back to spot her sister and the rest of the guests. A few were walking around on the boat, drinking. "We won't be far behind," he assured her.

"Mmm, okay."

The speedboat was docked. They walked in the sand with their feet sinking and holding hands. She was quiet but observant. He watched her slyly as she took notice of everything they passed. Didn't Cliff say she was a teacher of some sort?

"So what do you do?" he asked her.

"Do?"

"For a living, I mean. I think Cliff said you taught school. Is that right?" he asked.

She smiled. "College. I teach African-American studies at New York University."

"New York, huh? I thought you lived in the bay area?" He had assumed she did. He had just never bothered to confirm it.

"No. Grew up in Oakland. But I left. In fact I moved to New York and accepted my job right after the wedding."

"Oh, cool," he said and they reached the pier. "Here we are."

He owned a Baja two-seater speedboat. Equipped with a booming Jensen sound system and 320 horsepower. It was black with orange racing stripes down the sides and the front.

"There she is! Her name is Stella," he announced.

Deja brows lifted. "She's interesting."

"Interesting! She's a beaut!" He grabbed her by the waist and she gasped. He swiftly lifted her and put her over the side of the pier into the boat. Quickly he untied the vessel from the pier. Deja laughed playfully when he hopped in. "Are you ready?" he asked.

"I think so," she said.

He turned the key and reversed out into the water.

"So do you live in Miami?" she asked over the motor and the music blaring from the sound system.

"Sometimes. Got a place in New York, too." He gave her a sideways glance. She shook her head, smiling. Jon swerved and spun the wheel and sped out over the waters. The slice of the waves sprayed water along the sides and a bit inside the boat. But she wasn't one of those silly women afraid to get wet. In fact she tilted her head back and smiled.

"I would think you didn't like the water?" he asked. "Most claustrophobics don't."

"It's okay for me," she said. "I was forced into swim lessons and competitions since I was seven. Won several. But it was my mother who wanted the next Olympian. Thankfully my father saw how miserable I was at ten and put an end to it."

Jon understood. "Parents try to mold their kids into them, don't they," he said rather than asked. He slowed down on the speed and led them into a nice glide. He decided to take them west instead of east and circle back. Prolong the journey a bit. "My father had those kinds of expectations of me. First class all the way! He put me in the best schools, got me an Ivy League degree," he said, casting a wry smile.

"So why did you go into sports management? Was that his idea?" she asked.

Jon glanced from the ocean ahead to the beautiful woman next to him. "No. I did it to piss him off."

She chuckled. "Are you serious?"

He nodded. "Yes. Dad groomed his sons for hotel management. We're Hendrix men and expected to take the reins from him and lead the Hendrix dynasty into the next century. Or some bullshit. I wanted the opposite. Started my own business. Got ahead of a few draft picks before they knew better than to sign with me and I landed some good deals. The rest is history."

"Ah, well, I guess no matter what our parents wanted we are our own people, aren't we?" she smiled.

"Definitely. Look," he nodded to the sunset.

Deja looked up to the sky. The timing was perfect. The sun was an orange globe submerged halfway into the sea. It was visual poetry. She relaxed next to him while they watched the sun's descent. He switched the music to something bluesy and the lull of the boat was almost as seductive as the tips of his fingers light and gentle as they brushed her arm. When the last of the sun disappeared darkness engulfed them. Jon switched on the lights to the speedboat. They were alone.

"Where's the island?" she asked.

"Here." He tapped the navigation panel. "East. There!" he pointed out to the ocean.

"Can we leave? I mean go." She looked around at the vast open sea. He touched her chin with his finger and turned her face to look at him. The luminance from the control panel made his mouth all the more tempting.

"Are you sure this is the way you want to end it?" he asked.

"No. This is." She replied by brushing her lips across his. When his lips pressed against hers she felt the last of her defenses melt. He moved his lips down from her mouth to over her throat to trace his tongue where her neck and shoulder met. Lust was rising so fast and so hard in her she struggled to breathe. And then he touched her thigh, squeezed it hard as he traced his tongue back up her throat. Heat spread through her pelvis and sent tingles through her core. She rubbed her thighs together but the friction only made it worse. Deja touched his face and he brought his mouth back up to hers. She swept her tongue deeply into his mouth with the swirl and chase they lived for.

It was Jon who ended their passion before it began. And she was surprised by his actions. "I guess we're more than friends now." He stated rather than asked.

She blinked at him, stunned by the truth. Earlier when they had fought she had said she didn't randomly kiss men. A kiss had meaning. There was plenty to understand and own within that kiss. "We're family, remember? My sister, your brother?"

"Mmm?" he brushed his finger over her cheek.

"Is this the only reason you brought me out here at sea, alone?" she asked. "For another kiss?"

"Part of my reason," Jon replied.

"And the other part?" she asked.

"I told you. I want to know you. Why does that surprise you?" he asked.

She held her tongue. If he wanted to know her he could have made a move in the past two years. But why debate semantics. He was asking now, and here and now was all that mattered. "What do you want to know?" she asked.

"How old are you, Deja?" he asked.

"Thirty-six."

His brows lifted. "I'm surprised. You look younger, but act much older."

She chuckled. "Thanks, I think. How old are you?"

"Forty-two."

Now it was her turn to look shocked. She'd guessed him to be the same age as her. "Wow, I wouldn't have guessed. You look much older and act much younger," she teased.

He tickled her and she laughed, pushing him off her. The boat bobbed left and right hard and fast.

"Gee, thanks, I think," he said, chuckling.

They settled into a comfortable silence again. Deja looked up at the stars in the sky. There were so many. Some shone brighter than others.

"What does one learn in an African-American studies class?" Jon asked her.

"About African-Americans," she joked.

"Seriously, Professor. Teach me something," he said, looking at her. She glanced over and saw he was earnest.

"Hmm…well, typically when students sign up for my class they do so for a required elective. Many come in expecting to hear some boring lecture about 'the great achievement of black folks in America,'" she said, using air quotes.

"And that's not what you teach?" Jon pressed.

"No. I like to have dialogue. For instance," she turned a bit and looked into his eyes. "Did you know that studies say black women who are over the age of thirty-five, single with no kids, are least likely to ever marry?" she asked.

"Bullshit!" he chuckled.

"I'm serious, Jon. Let me ask you this, how many women over the age of thirty-five do you date?"

He didn't answer.

"Okay, that few, huh?"

He smiled.

"If you chose to date a woman over thirty-five what are the odds that she would be black?"

"Very high," he said. He gave her a sideways glance.

Deja chuckled. "How many women out of the over thirty-five group that you don't date are black?" she asked. "Generalizations about African-American women and their likelihood to marry or have kids out of wedlock have evolved over the years. At one time we were considered the greatest mothers and caregivers. Called upon to take care of wealthy people's children, even nurse them. Now we're the least desirable and last chosen for a mate? The class that I teach examines these studies and we separate fact from fiction."

"For the record I believe that's bullshit. The older men get, the younger they want to date. It's an ego thing, baby," he smiled. "Not the color of your skin."

"I know. My job is to make sure you do, too." She winked.

"Smart and beautiful. A deadly combination," he said.

"You like them dumb and blonde instead?" she teased.

"Just dumb," he said.

Deja shook her head. "What else is there to know about me? I teach, I'm single, I—"

"You have a strawberry tattoo. What's that about?" he asked.

"Enough of Q&A. Can we go please?" she laughed.

"Okay, but one last question."

Deja threw her hands up. "I got the tattoo from an ex-boyfriend when I was in college. He was an artist, a tattooist. Okay?"

He laughed. "No. I wanted to know if you'd like to drive, take us in?"

"Me?" she asked.

"Hell yeah, why not." He eased out of the seat and

climbed on the top of the back of the speedboat so she could slide over. She did so with ease. He pushed himself down into her now-vacant seat. "Okay. Press that button with your foot on the brake. Like starting a car."

She did as he instructed and the engine turned over. She grinned from behind the wheel. They bobbed against the rolling waves but didn't surge forward. Not yet.

"Think of it like a car. Steering, gas, all of it real simple. We're going to take a different route." He punched in the coordinates.

"Where's your brother's boat?" she asked.

"Ahead of us, I'm sure. They stopped to watch the sunset. But to make sure you don't come up on them too fast we'll go this way. Besides there are some reefs we can't see nearer to the shore. Hit one of them and it can split this baby like a banana."

"Is it safe? For me to drive?" she asked.

"Trust me."

"Okay. Okay!" she said, and steadied her grip on the steering wheel.

"Now on the count of three—"

"Three!" She yelled. She floored it. Jon was forced back against his seat. The speedboat glided over the waves. She managed quite nicely for twenty minutes into the ride. He had reclined and let the trip relax him. But after a long moment of bobbing over the sea his eyes opened.

"Slow down, sweetheart, you're picking up speed," he said.

"This is fun!" she squealed and turned the wheel so they cut east and then zipped out across the ocean going a full seventy miles an hour and climbing. She swerved west. Where was his shy, scholarly professor, he wondered? He began to appreciate her bold confidence.

"Hold on!" She sped straight ahead. He glanced down to the navigation panel and saw it blinking. He frowned. They were off course. The GPS indicated they were headed away from the private island, not toward it.

"Shit!" he said, trying to gauge their coordinates. He glanced up and saw the coastline of the island ahead. Jon frowned. Where where they?

"Deja! Slow down! Slow down, sweetheart!" he grabbed the wheel to steer her away from the unseen reefs. The blanket of night shielded them.

"Okay! I am slowing down," she said "I got it. Let go of the wheel!"

Control for either of them came too late. The boat hit something. He wasn't sure what because the next thing he knew they were airborne. He was thrown bodily out of the boat and crashed hard into the tepid waters of the sea. The impact nearly ripped his head from his shoulders. The pain was instant. He took seawater into his mouth and nostrils. The dark undercurrent roped his ankles and threatened to drag him into the abyss. Or so he thought when he panicked. Jon fought to swim to the surface. In a matter of minutes he breached the top. Jon coughed. He gagged. He could smell the engine oil in the ocean and see parts of the wreckage aflame around him.

"Deja!" he croaked.

Could she still be under? God help him, where could she be? "No! No! No! Deja!" he yelled. He turned in the water. Arms extended and legs kicking he kept afloat as rolling waves washed over him several times. He spit out water and tried to calm his panic. "Deja! Sweetheart! Where are you! Where are you!"

"Jon!" he heard a soft voice cry out from behind him. "Jon!"

He turned and tried to see over the waves. And thanks

to the moon he saw her hand wave up from out of the sea. "Oh, God! Thank God!" he nearly wept. He swam to her. He tried hard but the push of the ocean current steered him away from a straight swim. Three minutes in this struggle she swam up to him. She grinned so bright his heart nearly ceased to beat.

"Are you okay?" she rushed out in a breath.

"Me! Thank God you're all right!" He grabbed her up to him and they sank into the sea. They had to release each other to swim back up to the current. He turned and looked around. "The reef. We're close to the shore. Are you hurt?" he gasped.

"No!" she panted. "I'm just scared. I ache a little in the back. But I'm okay."

"Good. Scared is good," he smiled. "Let's go."

"But we can't see," she reasoned.

"We're close. We hit the reef. Swim away from the wreckage and we'll see the beach soon." He looked up to the sky and the moon. The stars twinkled. He was talking bullshit. He had no idea where they were. But his instinct said that they'd find the shore. So they swam and they did it together.

Chapter 3

Shipwrecked

Deja crawled across the sand. She gasped and choked on the salty water that had filled her throat. She had immediately puked into the sand. She had lost her sarong. Her hair was wet and loose, plastered to her head. After a minute braced by quivering arms she dropped exhausted in her bikini on the sand. But even in exhaustion she had to look for him. Jon was on his knees. He had his head down as if praying. His shirt was off and all he wore was his long shorts.

"Hey? You okay?" Deja wheezed and pushed herself up from the sand with her hands. She was able to turn and sit upright. It was as if the moon had grown brighter during their swim, led them straight to the shore. And because of its ethereal glow the beach was illuminated enough to give them some idea of where they were.

Jon managed to rise. He staggered toward her. He dropped on the sand next to her. "I'm sorry," he said softly. "You could've been killed. Damn it. What was I thinking?"

"It's my fault."

"What the hell happened out there? We were coasting and the next thing I know you went crazy!" Jon said.

She swallowed her sheepish smile. "I got carried away. But we're okay," Deja said. "In fact I feel invigorated."

He frowned and looked at her as if she had two heads. She chuckled. She waved off his questioning stare. "What I mean is I haven't swam like that since I was ten years old. Didn't know I still had it in me. Guess my momma could be thanked for that. And trust me, I don't thank her often."

Jon groaned. He looked around the beach. She cast her gaze left and then right. There was nothing but sand and, in the distance, a clump of trees.

"Where are we?" she asked.

"One of the islands. I'm not sure. I was trying to figure it out when we got close to the reefs."

"How did you know we were close to the reefs?" she asked.

"Huh?"

"Out there, before the accident you shouted at me to stop. How did you know? Did you recognize the area?"

"The GPS showed we were in a red zone."

She nodded. They sat on the shore trying to catch their breaths. And then she saw it. Something bobbed in the water close to the shore. "Look! Maybe the satellite phone or the radio or something?" she said. She got to her feet, dusted the sand off her hands and butt, and walked out to the shore.

* * *

Jon watched her. He had taken his boat sailing the last time he was out but it was only to circle Abaco and the other side of the island. He didn't remember reprogramming it. Were they back where they started? The reefs less than a mile from the shore indicated they could be. Maybe he should tell her? He looked back to the trees and then to her.

She was so beautiful under the moonlight. The white bikini she wore was a red-blooded man's dream. And she didn't seem scared or hurt. In fact she appeared more alive and adventurous than he'd ever known her to be. Hell, an elevator had her jumping into his arms for rescue. But a boat crash had her grinning and bouncing with energy. Jon wiped his hand down his face and smiled. This was the kind of woman he needed.

She dragged the cooler in from the ocean. He watched. She dropped to her knees and opened it.

"We have a first-aid kit! And some beer! What else do we need?" She laughed.

He pushed up from the sand and walked over to her. The driftwood was now floating on the surface waves. His baby was destroyed. When the sun rose he'd see the rest of it off the reefs. She smiled up at him. "If we had a tent or raft it would be perfect."

"Let's get off the beach," he said. He dropped next to her and picked up the little case that had the survival kit inside. He found a small flashlight. He turned it on.

"But we don't know where we are? What's in those woods? I think we should stay here until sunrise. Somebody will be looking for us."

"They will think we either went back to our rooms or a private destination. The sun just went down. I guarantee that the temperature will plummet." Jon glanced back to the woods. Something looked familiar. "C'mon," he said taking one handle of the cooler and the first-aid kit.

Deja lifted the other and they trekked up the sand. She used the flashlight to guide them and soon they walked through the trees and found a worn-over path. Ten minutes into the walk they stumbled upon a clearing. Deja lowered her end of the cooler and Jon did the same.

"Does someone live here?" she asked.

"Give me the flashlight," he whispered. She handed it over. "Stay here. Don't come out of the bush unless I call for you."

She nodded her agreement. Jon shone the light on what looked to be an empty cottage. The beam landed on the screen door and he switched to the black windows. He could see nothing more. When he reached the door he looked over to the left. He turned the flashlight to the sign that had been covered by vegetation. It read Blue Ridge.

Jon smiled. "I can't believe it, we're back in Abaco."

Behind the Oasis were several private bungalows. There used to be a cluster of them that they called Blue Ridge. Cliff had mentioned that they stopped renting them and had plans to do some renovations.

"Well, I'll be damned," he said, chuckling to himself. The place was completely safe and just a quarter of a mile from the resort.

"Jon!" Deja called out.

"Come out! It's okay."

She emerged from the trees and looked at him and the cottage curiously. "What is it?" she asked.

He opened his mouth. He had the intention of telling her the truth. But seeing her in the bikini under the moonlight, it hit him. If he ended the night and took them back to the resort the chance to keep her close and get to know her would be gone. She walked toward him and he struggled with what to do or say next.

"Do you know this place?" she asked.

"Ah, yeah, sort of. It's uh, it's close to Abaco, uh, the island, I mean. We're safe. In the morning they will find us easy. We can camp out here tonight."

"Really? Are you sure? It looks a little creepy." She stepped back and looked at the dark windows. Jon turned the flashlight beam on the place. The island was safe and relatively crime-free.

"Let me check for the lady," he said.

Deja watched as he disappeared inside. The cottage was raised at least four feet off the ground by cinder blocks. It looked old and abandoned. She had to reconsider her adventurous attitude. The more they walked in the forest the less appealing being stranded on an island was to her.

"We're good!" he said.

She yelped and whirled, nearly tripping over her own feet. Jon grinned from behind her.

"How the hell did you get around me?" she asked.

"I went straight through to the back door. Circled around to make sure it was safe. We're good." He gave her a curt bow of his head.

She laughed. She hit his arm playfully.

"Here, go inside," he said passing her the flashlight. "I'll bring in the beer."

She nodded and did as he said. The cottage was darker than the night outside when she entered. She could barely see in front of her. She heard him when he joined her. "How did you find the back door? I can't see anything," she said.

"You're holding the flashlight." He reminded her.

She chuckled. "Oh, yeah, you're right."

She turned the bright slender beam on him. He put up his hand to guard his eyes. "Shine it over there," he pointed.

Deja did as he asked. To her delight there were two gas lanterns. He walked up behind her and eased his arm around her waist. She was crushed to his chest. He kissed the back of her head and she loved the intimacy. "We have a lighter in the kit, don't we?" he asked.

"Yeah, I think so," she said, smiling.

He let her go and immediately she missed his comfort. She turned the beam on him to aid in his search. He found what he was looking for and then went to the lanterns and lit each of them. For them to still have gas inside meant this place couldn't have been abandoned for long. She pushed that thought to the back of her mind once the entire room flooded with light.

A wicker sofa was on its side, with cushions tossed about. Deja clicked off the flashlight and tried to right everything. There wasn't a fireplace and it felt cool inside. She did notice a table and two chairs so there might be a kitchen. The wood floor was covered in so much dust they had left footprints. The walls were wood-paneled and a faded portrait of an island scene was hung on one of them.

As she put the last of the cushions on the sofa she turned to see him go through a side door. Curious, she picked up one of the lanterns and went after him. Deja stopped in surprise. There was a bed. It was a canopy with sheer draping around it. A room fit for an island stay.

"Some of the islands have these bungalows as rentals, for honeymooners. There's a kitchen, too," he told her.

"It's nice. Do we have running water?"

He walked over to the bathroom and checked. "Yes!" He called out. "Most of the water reserves are from rainwater that is collected on the roof and fills the tanks for showering and using the toilet."

"That's quite economical," she said.

He came over to her. When he touched her face she stepped back. "You're hurt, sweetheart."

"Huh? I am?" she asked.

He touched just at her hairline and then showed her his fingers. The spot of blood made her brow crease with worry. "You must have hit your head in the accident, maybe on the reef. Does it hurt?" he asked.

"No. I, ah, I feel fine."

He took her hand and kissed it. He then led her from the bedroom to the front of the cabin. She sat on the sofa and watched a he dragged over the coffee table and opened the first-aid kit.

"So you're a doctor now?" she asked.

"I was an Eagle Scout," he said.

The timbre in his voice, the soft lighting and her exhaustion diluted her emotions. She couldn't believe her night. It was something out of a romance novel. Stranded on an island with her superhero.

"Do you know who you look like?" she asked.

He continued to dab at her cut with peroxide and a cotton ball. "Who?"

"The guy who runs into a phone booth and changes into a cape. You know who I mean. Not the old one, the new one. What's the actor's name who plays him? Colin Farrell?"

He chuckled. "Henry Cavill."

"Yes! That's him," she giggled.

"Do you know who you look like?" he asked.

She arched a brow and winced immediately.

"Hurts, doesn't it?"

"Stings, but I'm okay. Who do I look like?" she asked.

"Sanaa Lathan," he said, smiling.

She laughed. "I take it she's your favorite *black* actress?"

"Nope. She's your twin. Thought it the first time I laid eyes on you."

"Wanna make a movie?" she asked. "You be my superhero and I'll be your damsel in distress."

"Where is a man's camera phone when he needs it?" he chuckled.

"Ow!" she winced.

"Forgive me, love. Almost done." He finished tending to her wound and kissed her brow.

"Mmm. The kiss," she breathed.

"What did you say," he whispered against her ear.

"The kiss. It always starts with a kiss between you and me. First the elevator—" she opened her eyes and looked over at him "—and then the boat, now this. Kiss me and it goes down. We go down."

"But I didn't kiss you, beautiful," he whispered again.

"Oh, yes, you did. The definition of a kiss is lips upon skin. And your lips, sir, just touched my skin."

"So that means it doesn't have to be lips on lips?" he asked with his hand now gently caressing her thigh.

"Mmm…" She closed her eyes as the weight of the day began to crush her.

"Then let me kiss you again," he replied.

"Go for it…"

She puckered her lips and tried to suppress a smile. She was open to a sweet kiss from him before they went to sleep. To be honest she was open to many things with him now. His hand slowly eased over her tummy. It wasn't as flat as she wished, but thanks to her missed dinner she didn't have that little bulge she often got after a meal. She smiled. And then his fingers reached the tie to her bikini on her hip. Deja's lids flipped open and her eyes stretched. Jon untied the knot and freed the thin fabric. She closed her hands into fists to keep from stopping him.

Should I stop him?

Should I say something?

I thought he said a kiss.

Jon eased off the sofa. He was now between her thighs, which he parted with his hands. He removed her bikini bottom and tossed it aside. They both were grimy from the sand and water. She didn't feel at her best, but one look into his eyes and she knew he could care less.

"This is the kiss I've been wanting to give you."

He pulled her down on the sofa and she gasped. He pushed one leg up and apart by the ankle and in doing so spread the lips of her sex for his perusal. Deja felt the unyielding coolness of the room's temperature wash over her. His face lowered and so did her lids. The swipe of his tongue was tantalizing and sweet. It gave a lazy roll over her clitoris and then delved down to her opening. Every lick and glide of his tongue stoked the heat inside of her higher. Her thighs quivered. She bucked her hips and smashed her sex into his face causing his mouth and nose to bury deep. She gripped his head to keep him there. "Oh, baby, it feels good" she heard herself cry.

He was far from done. He licked her from top to bottom. He plunged his tongue deep and licked his way back up and delivered jolt after yummy jolt of pleasure through her body. Her toes curled as she pulsed with greed. She wanted more. Lots more. She wanted him. She gripped his hair with both hands. He pushed both her feet up to rest on the sofa cushion and her knees dropped further apart. She was his. Her sex now fully possessed by his wonderful mouth. She rolled her ass in timing with his

sweeping tongue and bit down on her bottom lip to sti-
fle the groans. And then it became too much. Repeated
gyrations up against his mouth with his hands on her
inner thighs pressing them down to keep her in place
unleashed something primal in them both. He fed on her
and she heard herself howling in pleasure. Screams and
whimpers that could be heard all the way to the beach.

Chapter 4

Paradise

Deja didn't feel very sensible. And considering what had transpired between them both she knew that was reasonable. He stood before her with an erection. Deja shivered below the waist with aftershocks. It had been months, close to years since a man had made her purr like a kitten.

"Still want to be my damsel in distress?" he asked.

"Anything for you," she sighed. He took hold of both her arms and brought her to her feet. The mere act of standing stilled the warm tingling below her waist and eased the tightness in her chest. But her legs felt weak. When she pushed at his chest, a bit light-headed, he took the gesture as rejection. He swept her up into his arms.

"Hey, slow down, lover-boy," she gasped and half chuckled.

"Too late for that, beautiful," he muttered. "We've already gone too far."

She couldn't believe he carried her. Did men actually still carry women to the bed? Where did he think she'd run off to? Deja gave a small, involuntary gasp when he tossed her on top. She was quick to undo her top. He dropped his slack shorts in a wet heap to the floor. Deja extended her hand to him.

"Don't tell me you don't want this as much as I do. Don't give me any excuses tonight." His voice had a gravel texture to it. But his eyes held a plea that she clearly understood.

"I'm out of excuses," she said to him. Her hand lifted from the bed. "I don't need them anymore."

He took her hand. She braced herself with a stilted breath as he crawled in between her legs. His large hands went underneath and his grip was uncomfortably tight. But she refused to complain. He lifted and she tilted her pelvis so she could feel the rub of her slick center across his hard length. Jon slowly trailed his tongue up the valley of her breasts. She gripped his strong arms and soon she realized the rest of her was shaking with anticipation. His mouth found hers again and his tongue sweetly slipped in between her teeth.

It was difficult to breathe. Not from the pressure of his chest pinning her to the bed. Not from the firm grip he had on her ass until his hands and knuckles were stark white. It was the anticipation.

"I want you," he said with his lips only a centimeter away from hers. "I don't have any protection."

She nodded that it did pose a problem. She not only didn't know his sexual history but she didn't take any kind of birth control because of her nonexistent sex life. So her problem was even more complex.

"Can I?" he looked down at her heaving chest. His gaze flashed up quick and snared her. "Have you?" he said.

She nodded that she wanted the same.

His hips lifted. The blunt head of his erection nudged her core. And with a single thrust he sank halfway in. She sucked in a strained breath through her clenched teeth. Hard and long she felt herself stretch and adjust to the invasion. Jon pulled out and thrust forward, rocking against her body. She knew she was tight. She could tell by the way he put an arch to his back and pumped his hips repeatedly. Delivering rapid strikes that had her clawing for mercy.

"Faster, Jon!"

The lovemaking stopped. Jon withdrew and she sighed over his retreat. He turned her. She crawled to an upright position on her elbows and knees. Jon forced her legs apart slipping into her once more from behind. Her vagina constricted and her nails scored the bedsheets and mattress. She felt him completely. The tap of his scrotum against her throbbing clitoris as he tunneled in and out of her left her biting into her pillow. Deja squeezed her eyes tightly shut. He thrust into her harder, and harder. He rode her and stroked her like a man possessed. She wheezed and rolled her hips and pelvis to ease the torment.

It was when he dropped on her and kissed her slick back while delivering several methodical thrusts that she lifted her face and cried out with happiness. Together they climaxed. But he kept moving. In and out, and over and over she felt him. His hand eased beneath her mound and he pinched her clit as he sucked the back of her neck. Deja shuddered, accepting the inevitable.

The ripples of her climax were so strong and overwhelming she felt his dick seizures deep within her. Jon gripped her by the shoulder with one hand and the hip with the other forcing her to her knees again. And this time delivered strike after glorious strike to her sex until every drop of his own was spent. They collapsed together.

Deja opened her eyes. It was dark and she was warm and content in her lover's arms. His face rested on her breast, his thigh was thrown across her legs. She stared up at the ceiling and tried to make sense of passion with a man that couldn't compare to anything she'd ever felt with another person.

They had made love.

It was true some women could have sex and think it meant love right after. She wasn't one of those women. Night after night she had submerged herself in his life. She read the gossip blogs. She'd searched his name on Google when bored. She'd even watched the red-carpet event at the ESPY award ceremony to see him and his date arrive. One kiss in an elevator had made her dismiss all her suitors afterward. If she were really honest this was more than a fantasy. She was in love with the mystery of Jon Hendrix and now she was falling hard for the reality.

He groaned. Kissed her breast. And then he rolled over to his side of the bed. Deja reached under the covers and touched her sex. She was sticky between the thighs and tender everywhere below. Sex without protection was a foolish thing to do.

She slowly eased from under the covers and walked on her toes to the bathroom. Without the lantern the small space was dark and unbearably cramped. But moonlight poured in from the ceiling windows to give her some light. She didn't need much.

* * *

Jon was drowning. He sat up in bed gagging on the air trapped in his throat. He blinked several times until the feverish nightmare abated. The rush of water in his dream came from the shower, not the dark memory of the boat crashing on the rocks. The accident was still fresh on his mind. He touched his chest and waited for his heartbeat to stabilize. And then his mind rushed to deliver a vivid recall of every minute he'd shared with Deja. He glanced to the shower. He heard her, the soft melody of her humming. Kicking his feet loose of the sheets he sprung from bed and marched over to the bathroom.

There was no shower curtain. He found her as she tried to cleanse her skin of the sand and passionate encounter they'd shared. She stepped right under the showerhead. The voyeur in him couldn't deny himself the pleasure of watching. Rivulets of water cascaded down her back and over the swell of her ass. She was lush. The woman had curves in all the right places. Not like the unnaturally thin women with fake asses and tits that he had bedded before.

To his delight his dick agreed with him. He touched it and found it rising to the occasion once more. Deja glanced back at him. She paused and then smiled. Jon walked over to her. "Let me do that," he said.

She nodded and handed over the soap.

"Where did you find soap?" he asked.

"Guess the other tenants left it behind," she replied. He rubbed the bar between his hands and worked up a sudsy lather. He set it aside. He began to caress the lather over her breasts, flat tummy and wide hips. She rose on her toes and captured his mouth. The kiss was a swirl of emotional reflexes with his tongue darting over hers and her tongue reaching and sweeping over his.

Deja wrapped her arms around his neck and he stepped

with her back under the spray of water. His erection was angled up and he positioned her over it before bringing her down. Thanks to her elevated position with her legs fastened around his waist he could feel himself go deep and deeper. He aided in the way she rode him. He worked her ass up and down on his penis and was careful to keep them steady. Deja dropped her head back and the shower rained over her face. The woman had the darkest nipples he'd ever seen. He loved black women. Their skin, the smell of them when sexually aroused and these sweet thick nipples he could suckle to sleep.

Jon turned her to the wall and pinned her there. He stroked her hard. He knew his body would probably deny him the pleasure of a repeat performance tonight. So he held back. Forced his groin to contain the rush and demand of a release. His scrotum drew tighter and the muscles in his thighs coiled with restraint.

"Yeah, babe, yeah," he said and licked her neck up to her ear.

She held to him and grinned. He was certain she had enjoyed him as much as he had enjoyed her. Someday soon he'd seduce her and take his time, giving her the pleasure she deserved. But his desire for her mounted with each passing minute. He had to be selfish with their lovemaking this time. Too much pressure crushed in his manhood and spine. He grabbed one of her hands and pinned it flat to the wall, and held her up with his other squeezing her ass tight. Jon exploded inside of her. Gave her every drop of his essence. First woman in six years he'd sexed without a condom. Deja Jones was the woman of his dreams.

"Look what I found!" she squealed.

They had located old robes to cover themselves with

in the cottage. She went in search of glasses while he opened two bottles of beer. He glanced back over his shoulder and she stood there smiling. In her hands she held a box of saltines and a can.

"What is it? Thursday mystery meat?" he chuckled.

"Nope. It's tuna and it has a good expiration date. You know, I don't think this place is abandoned." She looked down at the monogrammed robe. "Maybe it's a holiday spot for the owners."

"Come here, beautiful," he said.

She walked around the sofa and sat next to him. She handed over the can. And he eyed it while she opened the box of crackers.

"And exactly how am I supposed to open this?" he asked.

She blinked at him and paused. "Oh? I forgot to look for a can opener."

He chuckled and tossed the can aside. Deja fed him a saltine and then ate one herself. They were stale. Still, she savored the taste.

He let his fingers sink in to the wet spongy strands of her hair. She chewed and stared straight ahead. He didn't read any playful flirtiness in her manner now.

"Something wrong?" he asked.

She cast her gaze over to him. "Why don't we have a real conversation for once?"

"Real, huh?"

She nodded and swallowed. "Have you ever been married, Jon?"

The woman went straight for his balls. The one thing he never did with anyone was discuss his personal life or past. Women claimed to want to know more about a man but they attached too much meaning to things that had nothing to do with them. If he shared with her that he was once engaged and cheated on his fiancée, what would she think? He had made big mistakes in the past. He'd atoned for most of them. Why dig up all the bones now for the sake of conversation?

Deja wanted a response. Hell, he'd slept with her twice with no protection. He owed her a list of all his sexual partners. The problem was after Carrie Anne, he couldn't name but two or three of his regulars out of hundreds. He was seen with many celebrities but their publicists mostly arranged those liaisons and he filled the role of stand-in.

"Cat got your tongue?" she asked and bit into another cracker.

Jon inhaled, then exhaled. "Her name was Carrie Anne. And no, we weren't married. Engaged. She was a corporate attorney. Lived in Brisbane, Australia." The words rushed from him in a single breath.

"What happened? Why didn't you marry her?"

"She ended it with me. Said I wasn't ready."

"Why?" Deja pressed. Her poking and prodding at that old wound killed his mood.

"I wasn't. I…ah…" He sighed.

"What? Just say it."

"I cheated on her. Okay?" he asked rather sharply.

"Oh," Deja said and he heard the disappointment in her voice.

"She told me she could get over the infidelity. That we lived so far apart it wasn't a complete shock to her. But she thought I did it on purpose. She thought I wanted to sabotage our happiness. At first I didn't believe her. And after I lost her I knew she was right. So I've…kept my relationships light and unattached."

Deja didn't respond. He could have put a spin on the breakup, or lied. Maybe he should have said that Carrie Anne was the cheater, or she came down with some terminal illness. He could've manipulated the facts the way he was doing with the cottage they were held up in. Keeping from her the truth of where they actually were. But he didn't want to. Deja calmed him. She excited him. He felt possibilities and believed in them with her.

"Excuse me," she said. She stood.

"Wait a second." He took her hand and pressed a kiss to it. "I'm a bit screwed up." He forced her to sit. "My father thinks I'm hopeless. My mother pretends she doesn't see my issues and my brother makes more excuses for my faults than I do. I'm an adult, Deja. I know you took a risk on me tonight. I know you gave me something special. I want to know you. Really get to know you."

"Why?" she asked. "Will we date? Start a long-distance romance? How well did that fare with you and Carrie Anne?"

Jon smiled. "We will go at any pace you say. We'll do things your way. I'll earn your trust." He kissed her nose. "I'll make you trust me," he continued and pecked her lips with his. He pressed his lips to hers until she responded with the kiss he wanted and reclined on the sofa bringing him with her.

He kissed her neck and face. And then he whispered in her ear. "Tell me about you. Were you ever engaged? Married?"

She looked up at him and he could see her calculating the risk. She would have to decide how vulnerable she truly wanted to be with him. And then she smiled and the tension between them relaxed. He put his head to her breast and lay between her parted legs on the sofa listening to the soft rhythmic melody of her heart.

"When I was in college I came close. His name was Jin."

"Jin? That sounds Asian?" Jon said.

"Yes, he was Chinese. I went to UCLA. I've always dated in and out of my race. I just date who I'm attracted to, I guess. It's not a conscious choice. I've dated and loved black men, too. Oh, God, I'm rambling," she sighed.

"It's not rambling, beautiful. We're talking. Tell me what happened to Jin?"

"His mother," she said with a chuckle. "She took one look at me and the wedding was off. End of story. He made an excuse of having to return to China to work for his father's business and it not being the right time. But I knew he was lying. After Jin, I started dating men who weren't as scholarly. The music scene is ripe in California, but even more eclectic and diverse in New York."

"Wait!" His head shot up. "You telling me you're a groupie?"

Deja laughed and hit at him playfully. "Not the kind you deal with, I'm sure. I like musicians, you like bimbos!"

"Ouch! That hurt," he said, grinning.

"Sorry." She rubbed his arm to soothe his ego. "I've dated many. Even the drummer of the band Electric Snakes."

"Impressive." He kissed her breast.

She rubbed his back. "Musicians are floaters. Kind of like you. Hard to pin them down. So I've had a few long-term relationships with men who didn't necessarily want to be in them. And none of them broached the subject of marriage."

"And the elevator?" he asked.

"Excuse me?" she said.

"Sweetheart, I can't get our first kiss out of my mind. I remember everything about it. Your terror was real in the elevator. But you were fearless out there in the ocean.

Like some kind of Viking Queen. Hell, I had a nightmare about that shit. But you're just fine. Why is it?"

"I don't know. My therapist said I have control issues. She said in any situation I'm not in control I lose my balance. But let me drive and I'll take the wheel," she said, laughing. "When the boat flipped and I was thrown from it I went into the water and it all came back to me. I'm a survivor. Not for a moment did I doubt that."

Deja went on to explain her history with her mother. How Mom was the one to always push them and her father was the one to soothe them. They had all been shocked when her dad finally found his voice to end his oppressive marriage. Deja had felt relief when their mother walked out of their lives.

"Jon?" she said.

She heard his soft snores. Deja laughed to herself. She shook her head smiling. She didn't have the heart to wake him. Her sisters would be proud of her. For that matter her therapist would be proud, as well. People were flawed, and she should know that better than anyone. But this man made her feel alive again. Why not enjoy it, explore it, go as far as this feeling took her? Soon she drifted to sleep with him, a smile on her face.

Chapter 5

Daybreak

"Wake up," he said.

Deja opened her eyes. Jon sat on the edge of the bed staring down at her with a sly smile. She grabbed the sheet and looked around. The last thing she remembered was falling asleep on the sofa while holding him. She lifted the sheet to find her robe was gone and she was nude beneath.

"I brought you to the bed and made you comfortable," he said.

"By taking off my robe?" She smiled.

"Well I made me comfortable by taking off your robe," he winked.

He returned with a tray of banana and mango slices, tuna and crackers and put them on her lap.

"Wow! What's this?" she scooted back into the pillows so she could sit upright.

"You missed dinner. I made breakfast. All kinds of fruits grow around here," Jon told her.

She ate and nodded. He chewed and stared. For a long pause neither of them could speak what was on their mind. So she broached the subject first. "We have to get help. Get back to the island."

"Let's worry about that a little later. We're close. Trust me," he said.

She ate some more.

"I was wondering if you would stay a little longer in Abaco. Since this visit was supposed to be for only the weekend," he asked.

"Stay?"

"Sure. We can swim, fish, do a little parasailing. Really get to know each other." Jon's gaze turned toward the windows he'd opened in the room. "Just because the sun has risen doesn't mean we have to let go of paradise."

"Okay, I'm in between sessions at the college. I have the time. I'll have to change my flight and—"

"Don't worry about that. I'm Jon Hendrix, remember? I'll get you back home safely."

He leaned in and kissed her brow. She fed him a slice of mango and he sucked the juices from her fingertips.

"I found something," he teased.

"More food?"

"Eat, we're going for a walk."

Deja did what he asked. She gulped down the food, she was so hungry. They really should return to the shore and look for some way to alert people that they were there. But she didn't press the issue. She felt safe and protected with Jon. After eating and rinsing her mouth out in the sink she put on her white bikini. It was all she had. She found him pacing in the front of the cabin.

"Ready?" he asked.

"Where are we going?" she asked.

"You ask too many questions, woman," he said. He took her hand and led her to the back of the cabin. Together they left through the back door. The grass was dewy and cool under the bottoms of her feet and the soil felt the same. He walked her through a path she didn't see deeper into the forest and she winced several times when she stepped on sharp rocks and things unseen in the grass. A pang of anxiety surfaced. After all they didn't know the island. What if they got lost or fell and hurt themselves?

They cleared the forest. Jon had to move aside for her to see paradise in its morning glory. The sun had risen high. It beamed brightly down a cliff where a waterfall flowed into greenish-blue waters. Wildflowers in the colors of pink and yellow bloomed nearly from every bush. Deja let go of his hand. "It's beautiful. The most beautiful place I've seen."

"I found it this morning when I came out to pick some fruit."

She took his hand and squeezed it. "I'm so glad you showed it to me."

"I was hoping we could have one last swim. Before we left."

She laughed. "Sure. Me first!" she shoved him back and then dived from the edge of the rocks into the water. The cold crush of water she sliced through forced the air from her lungs. She felt exhilarated. She swam fast below the surface and broke through just as Jon did a somersault into the lagoon. She laughed.

Jon drifted to her and she was swept into his arms. They bobbed and turned in the calm waters. She wrapped her arms around his neck.

"Now do you see why I wanted you to stay? Play with me. Let's enjoy each other."

"I'd love to," she said and kissed him.

"Jon? Deja?"

Startled, she glanced up. At the edge of the lagoon stood her brother-in-law and two other men. Deja let go of Jon and waved at them. Jon, however, just stared.

"I've sent three search boats out to look for you and you're here?" Cliff frowned.

Deja swam over to him. She knew they would be looking for them but why did they have to come so soon? She climbed out of the lagoon and Cliff reached to pull her up the embankment. Another man with him took off his shirt and passed it to her.

"So you never left?" Cliff asked her.

"Left? Of course we did. We hit the reefs and our boat flipped in the water," Deja told the men. "We could've been killed. Jon saved our lives. We swam to shore and found a cottage for the night. We were going back to the beach to look for a sign of rescue. Weren't we, Jon?"

Cliff looked from her to his brother. Instead of seeming relieved, he looked incensed. He narrowed his eyes on his brother and took a step toward him. "What cottage?" Cliff asked. "Is she talking about Blue Ridge?"

"Yeah!" Deja smiled. "It's the one we found. It's abandoned."

"Under construction," Cliff clarified. "I knew you were an asshole but this is too much. Did you tell her you were marooned on an island?"

"What?" Deja asked.

"I was going to tell her. We were going for a swim and I was going to explain it to her," Jon said.

"Tell me what?" Deja demanded. She kept the shirt tightly closed over her bikini with her clenched hand. Her heart beat so fast it was actually in physical pain. Nothing they said made sense. For heaven's sake, she'd been in the boat. She'd caused the accident. They were marooned.

"You're in Abaco. You're just behind the resort. Oasis is the owner of Blue Ridge. You didn't get lost on an island. You never left the island. Not really. It was more like you circled it," Cliff told her.

She whirled around to face Jon for an explanation. The guilt in his eyes hurt more than the truth. Deja struck him. Before she could realize what she was doing, she had hit him. Never in her life had she raised her hand to another human being. Shocked and repulsed by her actions she stepped back. Who was he? Who the hell was she? Some ditz playing shipwrecked? How could she be so stupid?

"Deja…"

"Don't touch me!" she shouted through her tears.

"At first I didn't know, sweetheart. Hell, the accident happened. You were there. How could I know? But then I…"

"That's a lie! You knew we were going to hit the reefs before the accident happened. I thought I almost killed us. That this was my fault! You let me believe we were stranded because of me. Damn it. Was this all to get me in bed?"

"No! Deja, listen to me," he reached for her and she stepped back. She was humiliated. "I didn't know for sure. I swear it to you. But when I found the cottage I just wanted…for us to…hang out."

"Hang out? Hang out! No. You wanted to screw my brains out and play some game with me. That's what you wanted." She looked him over. "You're everything they say you are. No. You're worse, because I don't even think they would believe you could sink this low."

"That's bullshit!" he shouted at her. And this time he did seize her arm. His brother tried to get between them but he shoved him off effortlessly. Jon pulled her toward him and looked her in her face. "I don't have to play games to get anything in life I want. The truth is I wanted you and this was the first chance I had to make it a reality. Nothing that happened between you and me was forced. And I'm not going to let you walk away because of your insecurities!"

"Get your damn hands off me!" she shoved harder than she had intended and he let her go. But in doing so he slipped from the rocks and crashed over into the lagoon. Deja screamed in surprise. She and Cliff were at the edge in time to see Jon emerge unharmed. He glared at her. She glared at him. She shook her head in disbelief. "I've heard enough," she said, her voice choked on emotion. "Can you please take me back to the resort? I'd like to go, please," she asked Cliff.

"Deja! Deja!" Jon yelled at her.

"Now!" she demanded from the men watching. Cliff nodded and one of the men started off the way they'd come. She was led to a waiting jeep. She didn't bother to look back. She wouldn't let the bastard see her cry.

"What the hell is wrong with you!" Cliff asked when Jon pulled himself up over the embankment.

Jon grunted. He got to his feet and dusted his hands. "You ruined it!"

"Did you trick her to sleep with her?"

"I don't trick women into bed!" Jon seethed.

"Dad was right about you. Now I have to explain to my wife what you did to her sister. I want you off the island. Go back to Miami. Just get the hell out of here, Jon," Cliff said.

Jon sucked down a deep breath and dropped his head back. "We had an accident and I put us in a cabin to keep from trekking through the forest at night. Did she look like she was in trouble? Did she?"

Cliff stared at him.

"To hell with you. I'll find Deja and explain." He started off but Cliff pushed him back.

"Stay away from her. I mean it, bro! Stay the hell away from her," Cliff warned.

Jon glared after his brother as he walked away. He had to see Deja. He hoped it wasn't too late to fix what he had done.

Deja heard the knocking at her door as soon as she stepped out of the shower. The last person she wanted to see was Jon. She had cried tears of frustration until her eyes swelled shut while in the shower. Why did she keep throwing herself at men who had the intellect of juveniles?

"It's me. Please open the door," her sister said.

Deja pulled on a pair of jeans and a shirt and ran up the zipper. She opened the door. "I'm leaving, Dee. Don't try to stop me," she said before turning away.

"Huh? No! Daddy arrives today. We have the big dinner and I thought we could spend the day together," Dee said.

"I have stuff at home I need to get back to. I'll…be there when you deliver the baby, I promise."

"What happened? Cliff said you were on the island last night? He said you were in an accident? Oh, God, look at your forehead. Were you hurt?"

Dee touched the tiny Band-Aid on her brow and she winced. "I'm fine. It was my own fault."

"Can you please talk to me and stop packing? I want to know what happened between you and Jon."

Deja sighed. She focused on running the zipper along her luggage. She wasn't going to waste any more energy on trying to dissect the motives of Jon Hendrix.

"Deja," Dee took her arm and made Deja face her. "Talk to me. You're hurt, and not just physically. I can tell."

Without thought Deja hugged her baby sister and buried her face in her neck. "I'm disappointed. I thought he was a nice guy."

"He is, Deja."

"He's a lying jerk. Trust me on this," Deja said and wiped her tears away.

"All men can be jerks." Her sister laughed. "I could tell you some stories about Cliff that would straighten your hair, honey. Took some work to get that one in line. Believe me."

Deja frowned. "Work? I thought you two were destined. Cliff seems like a pussycat."

"We are destiny!" Dee said. "But relationships take work. Look at Dina and what she puts up with Darren. Men can screw up, they can disappoint you, but if you're invested you don't give up on them. We don't give up on people we care about. Do we?"

"Mama did," Deja tossed out.

It was the one thing she shouldn't have said. Her sister's smile faded and her brow dented with concern. This was why she should she leave. Her sour mood would just spoil the day's events and her sister didn't deserve that.

"Mama tried to mold us, all of us, including Daddy. She had in her head what a perfect daughter and husband were and she was wrong. Do you want to be Mama? Leaving? Not accepting people for who they are?"

Deja shook her head sadly.

"Talk to Jon. I know the trick he played on you with the island was stupid. But you have to ask yourself when was the last time any man you liked went through so much effort?"

Laughter escaped Deja. Dee came over and took her hand. "Say hi to the baby."

"Hi, little one!" Deja said and rubbed Dee's tummy. "You be a good girl for Mommy and Daddy until your birthday. You can raise plenty of hell when you get here."

The baby kicked. Dee laughed. "Stay, Deja. That's an order!"

"I have to go. Not just because of Jon. I just… I have work, you know," Deja lied.

Her sister gave her a disappointed pout. "Okay. I'll arrange the private jet to take you back to Miami. Promise me you will talk to Jon before you leave."

Deja winked. And Dee was gone. Her sister was right. She did purposefully push people away when they disappointed her. However, her little sister was wrong about her reasons. It wasn't because she was like her mother. It was because she was afraid of being hurt when rejection came. Risking her heart just never seemed to bring about any reward.

Jon felt better after a shower. He bounded down the steps rolling up his sleeves. He saw Dee first. She stood near the concierge desk. Several of the staff were touching and talking to her round belly. He found it weird how silly adults could be when near a pregnant woman or newborn baby. He shook his head, amused. Earlier he'd visited Deja's room. She was gone. Maybe her sister would know where she was hiding.

"Dee?" he said. She turned around and smiled at him.

He walked toward her. "I thought you weren't supposed to be on your feet?" he asked.

"Oh, I'm fine. The doctor said some light walking was okay. And yesterday your brother nearly carried me around the island."

He smiled. He loved her humor. "I guess you heard about me and Deja."

She gave him a single nod. The staff dispersed, leaving her to him. "I want to explain. I shouldn't have tricked her."

"Why did you?" Dee asked.

He took her by the arm and helped her to the nearest lounge chair to sit. He took the seat across from her. "I guess you could say it's in my nature to do things the hard way. I really like her. Was hoping I could explain myself."

"Well, you better hurry," Dee said and checked her watch. "She's already left for the airport."

"Left?" he shot to his feet. He looked to the door and panic seized him. "When? How long?"

"Thirty minutes ago. Cliff arranged for a charter plane to take her back to Miami and then she will fly to…"

He was out the door before she could finish. He grabbed the keys to a passenger van from a passing valet and clicked the lock release on the key. The van to the far left flashed its headlights. Once behind the wheel he cursed himself and his late attempt to set things right with Deja. If he messed this up he would never forgive himself.

"Ma'am, the pilot is ready for you," a tall dark-skinned man said to her. Deja smiled her gratitude and shut off her phone. She was able to rebook an earlier flight with Delta Airlines into New York. She'd have to catch the red-eye but that didn't matter. She just wanted off the island. Tonight she'd call her father and apologize for not being there when he arrived.

Deja wheeled her carry-on bag with her. The heavy luggage she had brought was checked in when she first arrived. At the very small private end of the airport she had to walk outside of the terminal across the runway to the Cessna parked and waiting. Halfway there she heard the loud sound of a car engine's fast approach. When she glanced over the top of her sunglasses in the direction of the noise she saw it was a passenger van. It was very similar to the one that had brought her there.

And the van sped straight for her. Afraid of its high-speed approach she froze near the wing of the airplane. And as soon as it came to a stop she saw the driver. Deja shook her head and started toward the ladder. The flight attendant stood ready to help her board.

"Wait! Wait!" Jon yelled running after her. "Wait, damn it!" he demanded and grabbed her arm.

She snatched away from him.

"Sweetheart. Let me explain."

"I don't want to hear your explanation. No need for drama about this, Jon." She stepped closer to him and lowered her voice. "You had your fun. It's over."

"Like that? Just like that you're going to dismiss me? Us?"

She looked him in the eye and made no attempt to reveal her emotions. Her sunglasses helped conceal her true feelings. "You humiliated me. No! I humiliated me. I looked like a fool to everyone babbling that we were marooned on an island. Believing we were!" she shouted at him. "I don't have time for games."

"Is that really why you're leaving?" He blocked her from accessing the plane. "Or am I your excuse?"

"I told you I don't need one!"

"Of course you do," he rasped softly. "Blame me, blame statistics on how you and I could never be anything, blame the man on the moon. But never blame Deja. Because to blame yourself, sweetheart, means you have to admit the truth. You're scared. I get it. I don't like trusting people, either. Sometimes, very rare times, you have to."

Shame, guilt, regret shivered through her. She closed her eyes and tried to force his truth from her heart. Nothing she could say could counter her truth. She'd already shared and told him too much. When his lips touched hers she could do nothing but open her heart to him. It was happening faster than she could've expected. When did fantasizing about this man turn to love? She lifted her arms and soon they were circling his neck as she returned his passion. He let her go. But not before she too claimed him, kissed him, felt what they shared again.

"Stay," he said softly.

Deja blinked awake from his seduction. Her heart sang yes. Saying yes was what she always did for men who never sacrificed anything in return. He was no different. She was no different. This time what she needed more than his touch and empty promises was for things to really be different.

"You told me that everything beautiful between us begins with a kiss," he said. "Can this one be about second chances? Give me a few more days. I want to make it up to you."

She shook her head no. "You told me that you would earn my trust, Jon. That you'd do whatever is necessary to prove we deserve that chance. Prove it. Prove to me you're the man I think you are."

He frowned, not sure of her meaning. She wouldn't give him any further explanation. She grabbed the handle of her carry-on luggage and wheeled it to the plane. She handed it to the flight attendant and then glanced back at Jon. He watched her with his hands in his pockets. She smiled at him. To her relief he smiled back. Maybe she was wrong about him. Maybe they all were. Only time would tell.

Epilogue

Let's Do It Again

"Okay, everyone, please, please take a seat!" Deja clapped her hands at the noisy cloud of students arriving. She had an auditorium of close to two hundred students and only fifty minutes to introduce her lecture and objectives. The students shuffled about hugging and greeting each other after such a long summer break. "Class! Your seats please!" she called out to them again by cupping her hands like a bullhorn so her voice reached above the noise.

She walked to the whiteboard and removed a marker. She wrote "African-American Studies 101" and her name underneath. She wasn't due back in the classroom until next quarter, but when she got the call to fill an open slot on the curriculum she'd jumped at the chance. Three weeks of moping in her apartment had been far too long.

When she left the island she had expected him to follow. He had the money and the means. She wanted the courtship. A grand gesture to prove he indeed was her superhero. When she searched every gossip site and blog for updates on his fast lifestyle they came up empty. She even broke down and called her sister who was expected to deliver the baby any day now. Dee told her they hadn't seen or heard from Jon since the party in Abaco. The game was over.

"My name is Dr. Deja Jones. I want to welcome you all to African-American Studies 101. I have a PhD in psychology and behavioral science. Show of hands for those who have been forced to take this class because they needed an elective?" she asked.

The students exchanged looks but only a few dared to raise their hands. Deja chuckled. "It's okay. In here we can be honest. We will discuss everything in this classroom and I will help you separate facts from fiction. Best way to do that is to do away with the stereotypes, the tropes, the myths and prejudices. Now. Anyone care to give me a stereotype for Africans brought to the Americas?"

No one responded.

"Oh, c'mon. Don't be shy. What is a prevalent stereotype that you hear about African-Americans?"

A hand went up. She pointed at the girl in the center of the room. "Go ahead."

"Black people are lazy," she said.

Deja nodded. "That is a nasty generalization. One of the worst. And it's evolved within American culture all the way back to the colonial years of settlement. If any of you have read the teachings of Dr. Patricia A. Turner she explores at length the origins of stigma in pop culture. In this class we'll delve into the cultural influence and achievements of people of color in America. From the teachings of Marcus Garvey, to the love of the n-word in your favorite rap songs. We'll cover it all. So those of you who were forced into taking an elective you should be happy you chose the right one."

Several students clapped.

Deja smiled. She turned to the whiteboard.

"What about black women!" a man called out.

She paused and looked back to the class. "Who said that?"

A hand went up to the back of the classroom. She tried to see the person's face and could not. The man wore a baseball cap pulled low to his brow.

"Okay? Do you have something to add?"

"Yes. What about the stereotype of black women?"

"Which stereotype are we speaking of?" she asked.

The class went silent. No one dared speak. Deja squinted to get a good look at the student.

"I hear they aren't really popular in the dating game. Last to marry. You know the statistics and stuff."

"Aha? Statistics?" Deja felt her anger rise. She had opened the can of worms on stereotypes so she couldn't very well get defensive now. But there was always one student in every class that aggravated her nerves.

"Black women being unwed is a very exaggerated generalization when you hold these studies up to the divorce rate amongst all women," she said, preferring not to go any deeper. She turned back to the board.

"Really? So are you? Are you married, professor?"

Several students turned around in their seats to see who spoke. Deja, too, was caught by surprise. She again stepped away from the white board.

"That is not open for discussion!" she said.

"I'm curious."

"I said—"

"Because I don't believe it, Doc," he said over her objection. The man who spoke stood from his seat. Deja dropped the marker from her hand. He stepped out of the back aisle seat and turned his baseball cap backward so she could see him. Jon wore jeans and a white-collar shirt. He started down the stairs toward her. "I believe in what I know."

"And what is it the great Jon Hendrix thinks he knows?" she replied.

"I know that a woman as special as you deserves a ring."

"This is my class," she said. "Don't do this here. Please."

The eyes of her students were focused on them. She felt their curious stares. Heard the silent whispers. Instead of giving her space he stepped closer. He stood directly in front of her. "Don't do this. I could get in trouble," she pleaded.

He looked her over. Deja bent down to check herself. She was wearing a very conservative blazer over a dark blue silk shirt and matching slacks. Nothing about her resembled the exotic flair of the women she believed he courted. Still his gaze roamed over her in appreciation as if he found her nude. And he touched her. His hand grazed her cheek. "Trouble?" he asked.

She nodded.

"You're already in trouble. Nowhere to run to, Doc. So what are you going to do now?"

"I—"

"Don't fight me."

"Jon."

"Don't fight me," he said softly.

She looked beyond him to her students and then back up into his eyes.

"Why don't we make a few new stereotypes of our own?"

Deja laughed. She dropped her head, smiling. "Where have you been? It's been weeks and you haven't called. No one has heard from you."

"Moving," he smiled.

"Huh?" He had her attention. She stepped to him. She put her hands at his waist before she realized it. "Moving where?"

"After your class is over I'll tell you everything," he whispered in her ear. Before he turned to walk away she grabbed his sides to keep him with her.

He looked at her with a question in his eyes. It was now or never. She wouldn't make the same mistake twice. She wanted him to know that she did want a do-over. She wanted the messy risks, and the soul-endearing rewards that a girl found with new love.

"What is it, Doc?" He lifted her chin and looked directly into her eyes. "Say it."

Deja cleared her throat. "You told me that everything between us always starts with a kiss?" she whispered up to him as her gaze zeroed in on his lips.

He nodded.

"Then kiss me, Mr. Hendrix."

"Aren't you afraid?" he drawled.

She arched a brow. "Of who? You?"

He chuckled. "Of having an audience. Everyone will see you, and they'll judge you. Make assumptions about us both."

Deja looked around his arm and saw a couple of students with their cell phones trained on them, filming their reunion. She didn't care.

"Try me," she said to Jon.

Slowly he drew her up in his arms until she was standing on her toes in her four-inch heels. He turned them sideways in a fluid movement so the class could get a good look at them. Deja's excitement was so intense she didn't know how she managed to suppress a squeal of delight. She lifted her arms to hold him. The class applauded. A few whooped at them. The noise was as thunderous as her heart. The kiss was a beginning. A new one. She didn't care about perfection or what others thought. She didn't care about the statistics. All she cared about was that moment. And that man. Her man. His tongue swept in and hers melted around it. She went weak in his arms as he kissed her deeply and she dug her nails into broad shoulders when she lost the ability to breathe. He tore his mouth from hers and she smiled up at him.

"I'll meet you after class," he whispered in her ear. She let him go and stumbled back as he turned and walked out. Deja laughed and shook her head, smiling. How the hell would she get through the rest of the day?

The New York midday blared with the noise of traffic. The weather was crisp and the sky clear of clouds. Jon waited. He watched the front of the building with growing impatience as students and professors came and went. His hopes for a quick and exciting reunion were dashed when it dawned on him he'd have to wait for her to finish her day. At first he circled the campus. When the wait became too long he parked illegally and prayed he'd didn't caught. He'd spent weeks preparing for this day and he'd wait even longer to have her again. However, each passing minute felt like torture.

After a while, Deja walked out the front doors. She glanced left and right with her curly locks swept across her face from the wind. Jon smiled. He expected her to dress sensibly considering her job as a college professor.

Yet Deja was the kind of woman that could make a plain shirt and slacks sexy. Before she spotted him he observed her beauty and recommitted himself to his mission. The past few days without her had taught him a lot. He wanted a woman who challenged him and made him a stronger and better man. Dr. Deja Jones was one of a kind.

Soon her gaze landed on him. Her eyes were wide and sparkling with expectation. Deja approached with her laptop bag on her shoulder and her eyes never leaving him. He greeted her once more with a kiss.

"I'm sorry I made you wait so long. I had to get through class and then wrap up a few things."

"Get in," he said.

"In?" she asked. She glanced behind him to the car he leaned on. "Where are we going?"

"Somewhere private. We need to talk." He reached and opened the door. She kissed his lips and then got inside. He closed the door and went around to get in on the driver side. His sports car only sat two. Once inside the car he felt a sense of calm. He'd rehearsed this moment over in his head for weeks.

"What's with all the mystery?" she asked.

"I wouldn't call it mystery," he said. "How about we say adventure?"

"Adventure? Oh, really?" she said, laughing. "You show up in my class after close to two months and then…"

"And then what?" he asked.

"And I want to know why now. It's been weeks, Jon," she said.

He nodded. It was a fair question. He gazed ahead as he navigated through traffic. "Back in Abaco, what I did, I…"

"Don't apologize again. It was my fault for jumping to conclusions. Hell, I even caused the accident," she said.

He glanced over to her. "I wasn't going to apologize. I'm not sorry for it. The time we spent together. I've had women, lovers, some of them even friends, but never anyone like you, Deja."

She glanced away and a nervous smile flickered across her lips. Jon returned his eyes to the road. "You told me that I should earn your trust. That's why I didn't call you at first. I needed to get my head together." He let out a deep sigh. "And my life."

"I checked the blog sites, the news stations, the gossip pages of magazines and you weren't in any of them. I called my sister and they said they hadn't heard from you," she said. He felt a profound sense of relief. She'd been looking for him, waiting for him. She hadn't given up on him. He'd feared that he'd return to her and she would have moved on. Or worse she wouldn't care to start over with him. That was why he'd taken the risky move of showing up in her class, forcing her to give him another undeserved chance.

They settled into silence. He drove past the speed limit, anxious for the conversation to continue in a more private way. And for whatever reason she didn't question him. She let him lead the way.

After a twenty-minute drive they arrived at his condo. He drove in through the garage and parked in his private space.

"This is your place?" she asked.

"It is," he said. He refused to give away any other information. He helped her from the car and walked her through the garage to the private resident elevator. She held his hand and stood at his side in silence. Jon inhaled the delicious provocative fragrance of her skin. When they left the elevator and reached his door he paused outside of it.

Deja glanced up at him and then to the door. Jon turned and faced her. He liked the way she met his stare now with bold confidence. Gone was the shy uncertainty between them. "I've relocated my offices, my life, to here," he said.

She glanced to the closed door and he turned her chin to bring her gaze back to him. "I've missed you, Deja. I intend to spend every day that I can to show you how much." He brushed his lips across her cheek. "You bring out the best in me, Doc," he said against her ear. She wrapped her arms around his waist and hugged him. Jon only released her embrace to open the door. He held it for her to enter. His breath was tight in his lungs, and his palms clammy with nervous sweat.

The natural lighting from the open windows cast few shadows about the space. But the rose petals that led a trail into the spacious living room were clearly evident. Deja glanced back at him and then continued on. Inside the room were several vases of roses and pedestals of candles that had yet to be lit. She stopped and turned to him.

Jon tossed his keys into the candy dish and came in behind her. "I wish I could have done this at your place, but I had to improvise."

"What is all of this?"

"Dinner, conversation, a chance to get to know each other again," he said. He blew out his breath and glanced around. This place wasn't like his other residences. This was him. He had a few sports memorabilia pieces on the wall and hardly any furniture. In fact, the roses gave his condo an appeal he hadn't seen since he had moved in.

Deja removed her laptop bag's strap from her arm and dropped it to the sofa. "Jon. We don't have to start again."

"You sure about that, Doc? We didn't part on the best of terms."

"We parted on my terms. I'm willing to come together again on yours."

Jon narrowed his eyes on her. He wasn't sure he heard her right. But the smile to her lips said he might have. She then removed her blazer and tossed it. Jon watched her, transfixed by her beautiful smile. Deja approached him. When she stood before him she reached and took his baseball cap from his head and tossed it aside.

"I've been waiting to touch you all day," he said. He moved his hands up her curvaceous ass and hips. They glided up her back and he drew her in. His lips bore down on hers hard and punishing. Gone was the tender greeting they'd shared earlier. He had rehearsed it in his head. They'd sit by the window and he'd pour out his soul. Tell her his fears, his dreams. Tell her that he wanted a life that wasn't filled with all the fake baubles of wealth that were spoils from his famous clients. But with Deja he never could find the words. It was when he kissed her that his heart was open and revealed.

"We should talk," he reasoned between licks and kisses to her mouth.

"Too long…it's been too long," she panted returning his kisses. "Talk later," she said as she loosened his belt. Jon swallowed hard. When his mouth met hers again he felt all his senses come alive. Her lips were soft, succulent and her breasts crushed against his chest. Deja released his belt and lowered his zipper. Her hand soon glided into his boxers and she stroked his erection. Jon groaned with his tongue darting in and out of her mouth. Before he knew it, he had her by the ass and was carrying her to his sectional sofa.

When they both crashed on top of the sofa Jon pulled back. He rested his forehead against hers, dragging in deep breaths to calm himself. "Sex with us is so good, Deja. I don't want to mess this up. We should wait."

"Jon, look at me," she touched his face. He lifted his gaze from her lips to her eyes. "I don't want anything or anyone but you. It's already too good between us for me to deny it. I'm yours."

A sly smile crossed his face. "Stay here, with me. Move in."

He expected her to reject the offer. After all they hadn't seen each other in months. He hadn't given her the list of reasons why. He hadn't done all the things a woman as special as her deserved. He was fast-forwarding to the end.

"Okay," she said, snapping him out of his doubts.

"You're moving in?" he asked.

Deja chuckled. "I told you. I'm never leaving again."

Jon smiled. "Damn, woman. You keep blowing my mind."

* * * * *

An unexpected tenderness

KIMANI™ ROMANCE

Sherelle Green

Falling for **Autumn**

BARE SOPHISTICATION

Sherelle Green

Elite lingerie boutique owner Autumn Dupree is a realist when it comes to relationships, yet she has agreed to be her sister's maid of honor. Then, unexpectedly, best man and nightclub owner Ajay Reed arouses a passion in her Autumn never knew existed, while the alluring temptress is awakening new feelings he cannot deny. Ajay hopes he can convince Autumn that they both need to take a leap of faith…

BARE SOPHISTICATION

Available April 2016!

"This story will make even the most skeptical person believe in fate and the idea of the universe working to bring two people together."
—RT Book Reviews on *A TEMPTING PROPOSAL*

HARLEQUIN®
™ www.Harlequin.com

KPSG4460416

What he'll do for love

SHERYL LISTER

Tender Kisses

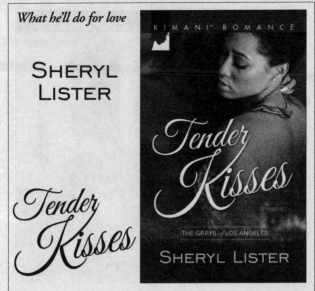

KIMANI™ ROMANCE

Tender Kisses

THE GRAYS *of* LOS ANGELES

SHERYL LISTER

Siobhan Gray is tired of men who view her as a career stepping-stone. When a sexy stranger sweeps her onto the dance floor at a gala, the twice-burned PR director vows not to let down her guard. Justin Cartwright plans to partner with Gray Home Safety to deliver his new cutting-edge product to the market. But can he convince Siobhan that nothing matters more than their blossoming relationship?

THE GRAYS *of* LOS ANGELES

Available April 2016!

"The author takes her time building up the passion to great results, allowing readers to vicariously experience the weightiness of their romantic journey."
—*RT Book Reviews* on *JUST TO BE WITH YOU*

HARLEQUIN®
www.Harlequin.com

KPSL4470416

Desire is more than skin-deep…

Sharon C. Cooper

KIMANI™ ROMANCE

Model ATTRACTION

Sharon C. Cooper

When an international modeling opportunity called, Janna Morgan answered, leaving her high school sweetheart behind. A chance encounter proves that Austin Reynolds definitely hasn't forgiven her, despite her regret. Yet their incredible connection reignites an undeniable passion in them both. But soon another can't-refuse offer beckons Janna overseas. Will it be déjà vu…or is their love finally ready for the spotlight?

Available April 2016!

HARLEQUIN®
www.Harlequin.com

KPSCC4480416

REQUEST YOUR FREE BOOKS!

2 FREE NOVELS PLUS 2 FREE GIFTS!

KIMANI™
ROMANCE

Love's ultimate destination!

YES! Please send me 2 FREE Harlequin® Kimani™ Romance novels and my 2 FREE gifts (gifts are worth about $10). After receiving them, if I don't wish to receive any more books, I can return the shipping statement marked "cancel." If I don't cancel, I will receive 4 brand-new novels every month and be billed just $5.44 per book in the U.S. or $5.99 per book in Canada. That's a savings of at least 16% off the cover price. It's quite a bargain! Shipping and handling is just 50¢ per book in the U.S. and 75¢ per book in Canada.* I understand that accepting the 2 free books and gifts places me under no obligation to buy anything. I can always return a shipment and cancel at any time. Even if I never buy another book, the two free books and gifts are mine to keep forever.

168/368 XDN GH4P

Name	(PLEASE PRINT)	
Address		Apt. #
City	State/Prov.	Zip/Postal Code

Signature (if under 18, a parent or guardian must sign)

Mail to the **Reader Service:**

IN U.S.A.: P.O. Box 1867, Buffalo, NY 14240-1867
IN CANADA: P.O. Box 609, Fort Erie, Ontario L2A 5X3

Want to try two free books from another line?
Call 1-800-873-8635 or visit www.ReaderService.com.

* Terms and prices subject to change without notice. Prices do not include applicable taxes. Sales tax applicable in N.Y. Canadian residents will be charged applicable taxes. Offer not valid in Quebec. This offer is limited to one order per household. Not valid for current subscribers to Harlequin® Kimani™ Romance books. All orders subject to credit approval. Credit or debit balances in a customer's account(s) may be offset by any other outstanding balance owed by or to the customer. Please allow 4 to 6 weeks for delivery. Offer available while quantities last.

Your Privacy—The Reader Service is committed to protecting your privacy. Our Privacy Policy is available online at www.ReaderService.com or upon request from the Reader Service.

We make a portion of our mailing list available to reputable third parties that offer products we believe may interest you. If you prefer that we not exchange your name with third parties, or if you wish to clarify or modify your communication preferences, please visit us at www.ReaderService.com/consumerchoice or write to us at Reader Service Preference Service, P.O. Box 9062, Buffalo, NY 14240-9062. Include your complete name and address.

KROM15

Turn your love of reading into rewards you'll love with

Harlequin My Rewards

Join for FREE today at www.HarlequinMyRewards.com

Earn **FREE BOOKS** of your choice.

Experience **EXCLUSIVE OFFERS** and contests.

Enjoy **BOOK RECOMMENDATIONS** selected just for you.

PLUS! Sign up now and get **500** points right away!

Earn **FREE** REWARDS

Join Today!

HarlequinMyRewards.com

MYR16R

SPECIAL EXCERPT FROM

ⓗ HARLEQUIN®

*After dumping her controlling fiancé, Chey Rodgers is
ready to live her life. Step one is moving to New York to
complete her degree—getting snowed in with a sensual
stranger isn't part of the plan! Successful attorney
Hunter Barrington has one semester to succeed as a
professor at his alma mater. He's put to the test when the
sultry beauty who shared his bed at a ski resort reappears
in his classroom. Will Hunter and Chey be able to avoid
scandal and attain their dreams of each other?*

Read on for a sneak peek at
HIS LOVE LESSON, the next exciting installment of
Nicki Night's
THE BARRINGTON BROTHERS *series!*

"Nice seeing you again…um…?" She pretended to forget
his name.

"Hunter," he interjected and held his hand out once again.

Chey shook it and that same feeling from before
returned—a slight flutter in her belly.

"Well—" she cleared her throat "—have a good night.
I guess I'll see you around."

"I'm sure. Probably right here in the same spot."
He chuckled.

"Oh. Sorry," Chey said for lack of anything better. "Good
night," she said again.

Chey didn't stop walking until she reached her villa. She pushed the door open, then quickly closed it behind her and leaned her back against it. Why was her heart beating so fast? Why was she flustered? Chey had carefully planned out her day and now that she'd had another encounter with the stranger—Hunter—she was mentally off balance.

Shaking off the feeling that had attached itself to her from the moment he touched her hand again, Chey headed to the first bedroom and pulled out her laptop. She decided to work on her novel. She booted up her computer and started reading through the last chapter she'd written. Every time she read the male character's lines, she imagined Hunter's voice, until finally she put the laptop aside and burst out laughing.

Chey lay back on the comfortable bed and savored the firmness of the mattress as it seemed to mold itself to her body. A vision of Hunter sleeping uneasily in that chair in the lobby popped into her mind. Chey closed her eyes tight in an attempt to rid herself of thoughts of him. She worked at this for some time before rising from the bed, bundling up and heading back to the main reception area to find Hunter, who was now "resting" in a new chair.

"You can have the second room in my villa on one condition."

Don't miss
HIS LOVE LESSON by Nicki Night,
available May 2016 wherever
Harlequin® Kimani Romance™
books and ebooks are sold.

Copyright © 2016 by Renee Daniel Flagler

HKMREXP0416